ALSO BY

AMÉLIE NOTHOMB

Tokyo Fiancée
Hygiene and the Assassin
Life Form

PÉTRONILLE

Amélie Nothomb

PÉTRONILLE

*Translated from the French
by Alison Anderson*

Europa
editions

Europa Editions
214 West 29th Street
New York, N.Y. 10001
www.europaeditions.com
info@europaeditions.com

Copyright © 2014 by Éditions Albin Michel
First Publication 2015 by Europa Editions

Translation by Alison Anderson
Original title: *Pétronille*
Translation copyright © 2015 by Europa Editions

Library of Congress Cataloging in Publication Data is available
ISBN 978-1-60945-290-2

Nothomb, Amélie
Pétronille

Book design by Emanuele Ragnisco
www.mekkanografici.com
Cover photo © Patrick Zwirc

Prepress by Grafica Punto Print – Rome

Printed in the USA

PÉTRONILLE

Intoxication doesn't just happen. It's an art, one that requires talent and application. Haphazard drinking leads nowhere.

While there is often something miraculous about the first time one gets really plastered, this is only thanks to proverbial beginner's luck: by definition, it will not happen again.

For years, I drank the way most people do: depending on the party, I consumed drinks of varying strength, in hopes of reaching that state of heady inebriation which makes life bearable, and all I achieved for my pains was a hangover. And yet I have never stopped believing that my quest might be turned to better advantage.

My experimental temperament gained the upper hand. I was like those shamans in the Amazon who, before they begin to chew away on some unknown plant, subject themselves to draconian diets, the better to unveil its hidden powers; I resorted to the oldest investigatory technique on the planet: I fasted. Asceticism is an instinctive way to create the inner void that is indispensable to any scientific discovery.

There is nothing more depressing than people who, when they are about to taste a superior vintage, express their need to "nibble on something": it is an insult to the food and an even greater one to the drink. "Otherwise, I'll get tipsy," they simper, aggravating their case. I feel like telling them they must not look at pretty girls, for fear of succumbing to their charms.

Drinking and wanting to avoid intoxication at the same time is as dishonorable as listening to sacred music while resisting any feeling of the sublime.

And so I fasted. And broke my fast with a Veuve Clicquot. The idea was to start with a good champagne, and thus the "Veuve" was not a bad choice.

Why champagne? Because champagne-induced intoxication is like no other. Every alcohol has its own particular armament; champagne is one of the only ones that does not inspire a vulgar metaphor. It elevates the soul toward a condition similar to that of a gentleman—in an era, that is, where that fine word still meant something. It makes one gracious, disinterested, light as air yet profound at the same time; it exalts love and confers elegance upon the loss of love. On these grounds I reasoned that here was an elixir that might turn my quest to better advantage.

And with the first sip I knew I was right: never had champagne tasted so exquisite. My thirty-six hours of fasting had sharpened my taste buds, and they detected even the faintest flavors in the alloy, quivering with a new sensual delight that started out virtuoso, quickly became brilliant, and ended transfixed.

Courageously, I continued drinking, and as I emptied the bottle I felt that the experience was changing in nature: what I attained did not deserve to be called intoxication so much as what is pompously referred to in today's scientific parlance as "a heightened state of consciousness." A shaman would have qualified it as a trance; a druggie would have called it a trip. I began to have visions.

It was six thirty in the evening, night was falling all around me. I looked into the darkest place and I saw, and heard, jewels. Their multiple fragments tinkled with precious gems, with gold and silver. Fragments that were animated by a serpentine crawling: they did not seek out the necks, wrists, or fingers they should have adorned, they were sufficient unto themselves and proclaimed the absolute nature of their luxury. As they approached me, I could feel their metallic chill. I felt the rapture of snow; I would have liked to bury my face in this frozen treasure. The most hallucinatory moment was when the palm of my hand actually felt the weight of a gemstone.

I let out a cry, which immediately dispelled the vision. I drank another glass and I understood that the potion was producing visions that resembled it: its golden color flowed into bracelets; its bubbles into diamonds. Every ice-cold sip brought a silvery chill.

The next stage was thought—if one can even qualify the current that bore my mind away as thought. At the opposite extreme from the ruminations which frequently bog it down, my mind began to twirl, to sparkle, to bluster with the most ethereal things: it was as if it sought to charm me. This was so unusual that I laughed out loud. I am so used to its recriminations, as if it were some tenant outraged by the shoddy quality of an apartment.

To be suddenly such pleasant company for my own self—this opened up new horizons. I would have liked to be similarly good company for someone. But for whom?

I went through all my acquaintances, among whom

there were a good number of likeable souls. But there were none who suited the occasion. What I needed was some-one who would agree to submit to extreme asceticism then drink with equal fervor. I could hardly subscribe to the notion that my ramblings might entertain a practitioner of sobriety.

In the meantime I had emptied the bottle and was dead drunk. I got to my feet and tried to walk; my legs marveled at the fact that under normal circumstances such a com-plicated dance would require no effort. I staggered to my bed and collapsed.

What an enchanting loss of self. I understood that the spirit of champagne approved of my behavior: I had wel-comed it into my body as if it were an honored guest, I had shown it the highest regard, and in exchange it was show-ering me with its virtues. Until this final shipwreck, there was nothing that had not been a favor. If Ulysses had thrown caution to the winds and chosen not to lash him-self to the mast, he would have come with me to the place where the ultimate power of the potion was leading, and he would have sunk with me to the bottom of the ocean, lulled by the golden chant of the Sirens.

I do not know how long I dwelled in that abyss, in a realm somewhere between sleep and death. I expected to feel comatose upon awakening, but I didn't. When I emerged from my depths, I discovered yet another sensual delight: I was now made painfully aware of the slightest details of the comfort around me, as if I had been crystal-lized in sugar. The touch of clothing on my skin caused me to quiver, the bed that supported my frail self propagated a promise of love and understanding right to the marrow. My mind was marinating in a pool bubbling with ideas, in

the etymological sense: an idea is first and foremost something one sees.

Thus, I could see that I was Ulysses, post-shipwreck,
washed up on some unknown shore, and before I could
draw up a plan I delighted in my astonishment at having
survived, at having all my organs in one piece, along with
a brain that was no worse affected than before, and that I
now lay upon the solid part of the planet. My Parisian
apartment was that unknown shore and I resisted the urge
to go to the toilet, to preserve a moment longer my curios-
ity with regard to the mysterious tribe that I would surely
meet there.

Upon reflection, that was the sole imperfection in my
state: I would have liked to share it with someone.
Nausicaa or the Cyclops would have fit the bill. Love or
friendship would be ideal resonance chambers for so
much wonder.

"I need a drinking companion," I thought. I went
through the list of people I knew in Paris, for I had only
recently moved there. My few connections included people who were either extremely nice, but did not drink
champagne, or real champagne drinkers who did not
appeal to me in the least.

I managed to visit the bathroom. When I came back, I
looked out the window at the restricted view of Paris there
below me: pedestrians trudging through the dark shadows
in the street. "Those are Parisians," I thought, examining
them as an entomologist would. "It seems impossible that
with so many people out there I cannot find the Chosen
One. In the City of Light, there must be someone with
whom I can drink the Light."

I was a thirty-year-old novelist who had recently moved to Paris. Booksellers invited me to come and do signings, and I never turned them down. People thronged to the bookstores to see me, and I greeted them with a smile. "How nice she is," they would say.

In fact, in a passive sort of way, I was on the prowl. As I had fallen prey to my curious readers, I studied them all, and wondered what each of them would be like as a drinking companion. My own predatory attitude was ever so risky, because, in the end, how could I identify such an individual?

For a start, the word "companion" was all wrong: its etymology signifies the sharing of bread. It was a *comvinion* I needed. Some of the booksellers took the happy initiative to serve me wine, or even champagne, which allowed me to assess any flicker of desire in a customer's eye. I liked it when they cast covetous looks at my glass, provided their gaze was not too intent.

The business of book signing is founded on a fundamental ambiguity: no one knows what the other person expects. How many journalists have asked me, "What do you hope to gain from this sort of encounter?" In my opinion, the question is even more pertinent when it applies to the other side. With the exception of the occasional fetishist for whom an author's signature really matters, what are these autograph hunters looking for? And as for me, I am extremely curious about the people who come to see me. I try to find out who they are and what they want. And this will never cease to fascinate me.

Nowadays it is slightly less of a mystery. I am not the only one who has observed that the prettiest girls in Paris stand in line to meet me, and it amuses me no end that many people will come to a signing for the opportunity it offers to chat up one of these young beauties. And the circumstances are ideal: I am excruciatingly slow in writing my dedications, so the players have all the time in the world.

My story begins in late 1997. In those days, the phenomenon was less obvious, if for no other reason than I had fewer readers in those days, which reduces *ipso facto* the likelihood of such dreamlike creatures being found among them. Those were heroic times. Booksellers did not serve much champagne. I did not yet have an office at my publisher's. I think back on this period with the same mixture of fear and emotion as does our species when remembering prehistoric times.

At first glance, I thought she looked so terribly young that I mistook her for a fifteen-year-old boy. Her youthfulness was confirmed by the exaggerated intensity of her eyes: she was staring at me as if I were the skeleton of the Glyptodon at the Jardin des Plantes.

I am read by a good number of adolescents. When the lycée has imposed one of my books on its pupils, it makes for only moderately interesting reading. But when kids themselves take the initiative to read me—now *that* is fascinating. And so I greeted the boy with genuine enthusiasm. He was on his own, proof that it wasn't a teacher who had sent him.

He handed me a copy of *Loving Sabotage*. I opened it to the flyleaf and uttered the ritual phrase: "Good evening. Who would you like me to make it out to?"

"Pétronille Fanto," answered a voice that was quite gender neutral, although slightly more feminine than masculine.

I was startled, not so much by my discovery of the individual's true gender as by her identity.

"It's you!" I cried.

How many times when signing have I experienced this moment: there before me stands someone with whom I have been corresponding. It is always such a shock. To go from an encounter on paper to an encounter in the flesh implies a complete change of dimension. I don't even know if it means going from the second to the third dimension, because perhaps it is the opposite. Often when I meet the actual correspondent, there is a regression, and I lapse into platitudes. And the awful thing is that this is irremediable: if the other person's appearance, for God knows whatever reason, does not match the loftiness of our correspondence, then our correspondence will never attain that level again. It is impossible to forget or to disregard. Or impossible for me, at any rate. Which is absurd, because there is nothing remotely romantic about these exchanges. It would be an error to think that looks are only important where love is concerned. For the majority of people, myself included, looks also matter in friendship, and even in the most elementary relationships. I'm not referring to beauty or ugliness, but rather to that thing that is so vague and so vital and which we call physiognomy. Right from the start, there are those with whom we feel great affinity, and other unlucky individuals whom we simply cannot stand. To deny this would only compound the injustice.

Of course, this can change: there are some people whose appearance is off-putting but who are so wonderful that you can learn to live with it, or even learn to like the way they look. And the reverse also holds true: people with particularly good looks gradually begin to lose their charm if we do not care for their personality. Regardless, we have to come to terms with this basic premise. And the moment we meet is the moment we suddenly take the measure of the other person's physical attributes.

"It's me," answered Pétronille.

"You're not how I imagined," I could not help but say.

"How did you imagine me?" she asked.

Which she was bound to say, after my idiotic declaration. In fact I had not imagined her one way or the other. When you are corresponding with someone, it's not an image you form so much as a vague intuition of the recipient's appearance. Pétronille Fanto, over the last three months, had sent me two or three handwritten letters in which she had not told me her age. She had written such deep, tenebrous things that I thought I must be dealing with someone who was approaching old age. And here I was face to face with a teenager with a chili pepper gaze.

"I thought you were older."

"I'm twenty-two," she said.

"You look younger."

She rolled her eyes, visibly annoyed, and this made me want to laugh.

"What do you do in life?"

"I'm a student," she said, and no doubt to curtail the obvious follow-up question, she added, "I'm doing a master's in Elizabethan literature. I'm writing my dissertation on one of Shakespeare's contemporaries."

"Remarkable! Which contemporary might that be?"

"You wouldn't know him," she answered, perfectly composed.

I burst out laughing.

"And you find the time to read my books between Marlowe and John Ford?"

"I'm allowed to have fun from time to time."

"I'm pleased to be your entertainment," I said, to conclude.

I would gladly have gone on talking to her, but she was not the last one in line. Each encounter with a reader must be brief, which more often than not is a relief. I wrote a few words on the title page of her copy of *Loving Sabotage*. I have no idea what I might have written. Without exception, what matters to me at a book signing is certainly not the actual signing.

There are two attitudes possible among the people whose book I have just signed: either they go away with their booty, or they go off to one side to watch me until the end of the session. Pétronille stayed and watched. I felt as if she were planning to make a wildlife documentary about me.

The signing was held at that marvelous, tiny bookshop in the seventeenth arrondissement, L'Astrée, at 69 Rue de Lévis. Michèle and Alain Lemoine always welcomed authors and readers with disarming kindness. As it was already very cold out on that late October night, they offered everyone a glass of mulled wine. I was enjoying my drink, and I noticed that Pétronille was not exactly ignoring her own glass.

She really did look like a fifteen-year-old boy: even her long hair, held back in an elastic, was like an adolescent's.

Suddenly up came a professional photographer who started snapping away without asking my permission. To keep from getting annoyed, I pretended I hadn't noticed his little game and I went on meeting my readers. Before long the lout was no longer content with merely being ignored and he started waving at people to move to one side. Smoke was pouring from my ears and I interceded:

"*Monsieur*, I am here for my readers, not for you. Therefore you have no business giving orders to anyone."

"I'm working for your fame and fortune," said the sycophant, continuing to snap away.

"No, you are working for your own bank account, and you are rude. You have already taken plenty of pictures. That's enough."

"This is a violation of freedom of the press!" said the man, establishing his true identity as a paparazzo.

Michèle and Alain Lemoine were horrified by what was going on in their bookstore (named for a seventeenth-century novel), yet they did not dare intercede. In the end it was Pétronille who grabbed the fellow by the scruff of the neck and dragged him outside with unswerving determination.

I never found out what happened, exactly, but I did not see the snap-happy scoundrel again, and none of his photographs turned up in the press.

No one mentioned the incident. I went on signing books with a smile. And then the booksellers, a few faithful customers and I finished off the mulled wine and chatted. I said good night, and headed for the Métro station.

Because it was dark, initially I did not see the little figure waiting for me at the end of the Rue de Lévis.

"Pétronille!" I exclaimed, surprised.

"What, did you think I was stalking you?"

"No. Thank you for dealing with the photographer. What did you do to him?"

"I told him what I thought. He won't bother you again."

"You sound like a character in a Michel Audiard film."

"If I write to you, will you still answer?"

"Of course."

She shook my hand and vanished into the night. I went down into the Métro, enchanted by our encounter. Pétronille seemed worthy of the Shakespearean contemporaries she was studying: bad boys who were always ready for a fight.

In this instance, my acquaintance with the letter writer's appearance did not adversely affect our correspondence. As I reread the letters of that dark, aging philosopher, Pétronille Fanto, the knowledge that they had been written by a pugnacious little boy with sparkling eyes gave them incredible piquancy.

A thought occurred to me: might Pétronille be the ideal comvinion? Yet I could not just come straight out and ask her what she might be like as a drinking companion. So I wrote to thank her for getting me out of an awkward situation, and invited her for a drink at Le Gymnase. I set a date and a time. She accepted by return mail.

Le Gymnase is a seedy café where I often go simply because it is located a hundred yards from my publisher's. I've always found this downmarket place extremely likeable—it is the archetypal Parisian bistro. On the counter you'll find a basket full of croissants, and one of those little round racks with hard-boiled eggs. The regulars are just as you would imagine, engaged in friendly arguments at the *zinc*.

It was the first Friday in November, at six in the evening. I got there first, as I always do: I am biologically incapable of not showing up at least ten minutes early. I like to get the feel of the ambient crowd before I devote myself to one person in particular.

While I tend to dress up like a Martian pagoda for my signing sessions, in this instance I was wearing my everyday black work duds: a long black skirt, an ordinary black jacket, and my black ruff, without which I would not be who I am—I staunchly support the return of the ruff, yet despite my fame I have never managed to win a single person over to my cause. Pétronille Fanto, as on the previous occasion, was wearing jeans and a leather jacket.

"I'll have a coffee," she said.

"Are you sure? Why don't we have something a bit more festive?"

"A half-pint of beer, then."

"I was thinking of champagne."

"Here?" said Pétronille, opening her eyes wide.

"Yes. It's fine here."

She looked all around, as if she'd missed something.

"Okay, then, here."

"Don't you like champagne?"

"Me, not like champagne?" she said indignantly.

"I didn't mean to offend you."

"Have you ever tried the champagne here?"

"No. This will be the opportunity."

"Do they even have any?"

"With the exception of the station buffet in Vierzon, there is champagne to be had everywhere in France."

Pétronille motioned to the waiter.

"Do you have champagne?"

"Yup. Two glasses?"

"A bottle, please," I said.

Pétronille and the waiter looked at me with newfound respect.

"I have some Roederer Brut," he said. "Sorry, no Cristal. Will that do?"

"Fine, provided it's chilled."

"But of course," he replied, shocked.

France is that magical country where at any time even the lowliest tavern knows how to serve a fine champagne at an ideal temperature.

While the good man was preparing our order, Pétronille said, "Do you have something to celebrate?"

"Yes. Our acquaintance."

"You shouldn't. It's not that important."

"Not to you—I can see why. But to me it is."

"Oh. Right."

"It's the beginning of a friendship."

"If that's where you're headed…"

"I hope so, in any case."

The waiter came back with two champagne flutes and a bottle in an ice bucket.

"Shall I open it?"

"Allow me," said Pétronille.

She casually popped the cork on the Roederer and filled the glasses.

"To our friendship!" I said solemnly.

The Roederer had that flavor which Imperial Russia attributed to French luxury: my mouth filled with the taste of happiness.

"Not bad," said Pétronille.

I observed her. She shared my exaltation. I appreciated the fact that she wasn't trying to act blasé.

The waiter brought some peanuts, which indicated a

strange sense of values. You might as well listen to the "Chicken Dance" while reading Turgenev. To my relief, Pétronille didn't touch them.

I have a tendency to drink quickly, even when it's excellent. It's not the worst way there is to honor a good drink. No champagne has ever faulted me for my enthusiasm, which absolutely does not reflect a lack of attention on my part. If I drink quickly, it is also so that the elixir doesn't have time to get warm. And not to hurt its feelings: the sparkling wine must not get the impression that my desire is lacking in urgency. Drinking quickly does not mean guzzling. Just one sip at a time, but I do not keep the magic potion in my mouth for long: I tend to swallow it when its icy edge is still almost painful.

"You should see your face," said Pétronille.

"It's because I'm concentrating on the champagne."

"You look weird when you concentrate."

I got her talking. With the help of the champagne, she confessed that her dissertation was on a play by Ben Jonson.

She had spent the last two years in Glasgow, where she had taught French in a secondary school. While she described her life in Scotland, a grim expression spread over her face: I concluded that she'd been in love there, and that it had ended badly.

I refilled our glasses. As the bottle emptied, we went back in time. She had grown up in the Paris suburbs. Her father was an electrician, her mother, a nurse at the hospital for the Paris transport system.

I was staring at her with the dumb admiration common to people of my sort when they meet a genuine proletarian.

"My father used to spend Sunday morning selling *L'Humanité* at the market."

"You're a communist!" I exclaimed enthusiastically: I had indeed found a rare pearl.

"Don't get carried away. My parents are communists, and I'm on the left, but I'm not a communist. I guess you're pretty upper-class, right?"

"I'm from Belgium," I said, to curtail the investigation.

"Yeah. That's okay, I get you."

She held out her flute for me to fill it.

"You're like me, you can knock it back," I said.

"What's it to you?"

"Nothing! I just like to drink with people who share my passion."

"Why don't you just say that you think it's fun to go slumming."

I looked at her closely, wondering if she was serious.

"Are you going to start up with the class struggle and dialectical materialism?" I asked. "When I invited you, I didn't know the first thing about your background."

"Your caste senses these things."

"I am not obsessed with 'these things,' as you put it."

The tension was rising. Pétronille must have realized, and she calmed down.

"In any case, we've found common ground," she said, indicating the bottle with her chin.

"Indeed we have."

"My parents like a good champagne. Not often, but we do drink it. A German invented communism, and the Russians put it into practice, and those are both countries that know how to appreciate good champagne."

"I was born in an embassy, so that's as good as being born in champagne."

"So you don't even notice what's exceptional about it anymore."

"Oh, you're wrong there. I've known splendor in my life, but misery, too. Do you often write to authors?"

"You're the first and so far the only one."

"To what do I owe the honor?"

"You make me laugh. I heard you on the radio. I didn't know who you were but I couldn't stop laughing. You were talking about how to milk a whale. And you said that you slip the word '*pneu*'—as in a rubber tire—into every one of your books. I read them all just to make sure, and you weren't lying."

"Which just goes to show that I give people serious reasons to read me."

"I liked your books. They touched me."

"I'm glad to hear that, thank you."

I wasn't just being polite. When someone likes my books, I am sincerely happy. Coming from the mouth of this strange gamine who terrorized photographers and hobnobbed with Shakespeare's contemporaries, the compliment was all the more enchanting.

"You must be used to it."

"I never get used to it. And besides, you're not just anyone."

"I suppose you're right. I'm difficult. I've tried to read contemporary authors, and I just get bored with them."

I tried to persuade her that she was wrong, and began to sing the praises of a multitude of living authors.

"None of them can hold a candle to Shakespeare," she said.

"Nor can I."

"You invite your readers to drink champagne, that's different."

"You had no way of knowing that. And besides, I don't do it with all my readers."

"I should hope not. I'll keep an eye on you."

I laughed, not altogether sincerely, because I thought she really might. She must have read my thoughts because she added, "Don't worry, I have far more important things to do with my life."

"I am sure you do. I would love to hear about them."

"You'll see."

Tipsiness helping, I could imagine her brilliant exploits: stealing the Crown Jewels on behalf of Scottish workers, or staging *'Tis Pity She's a Whore* at the Comédie-Française.

Pétronille must have had a certain flair for drama, because at that very moment she got to her feet.

"We're out of champagne," she said. "Why don't we go to the Montparnasse cemetery, it's at the end of the street."

"Excellent idea," I said. "We're bound to run into somebody interesting."

We hadn't reckoned with the early closing of Paris cemeteries in winter: the gates were shut. We headed back the other way along the Rue Huyghens toward the Boulevard Raspail. We must have gone about halfway when Pétronille informed me that she was going to urinate there on the spot, between two parked cars.

"Can't you wait until Le Gymnase?" I protested. "We've only got another thirty yards or so to go."

"Too late. Cover me."

Panic. What was I supposed to do? It was dark, with

thick clouds. You couldn't see fifty feet ahead of you on the sidewalk on the Rue Huyghens. In this atmosphere straight out of *Macbeth*, I was supposed to protect the privacy of this young person who, for reasons that partially escaped me, had read all my novels.

I listened out for any footsteps; all I could hear was the sound of a pee that seemed determined never to stop. My heart was pounding. I prepared my speech, in the event a passerby came our way: "Forgive me, sir, madam, my friend has had to answer an urgent call of nature, she won't be long, I do hope you won't mind waiting for a second, please?" What effect would my words have? I never got the chance to find out, because the little ditty came to an end a few seconds later; Pétronille reappeared.

"That's better," she said.

"I'm delighted to hear it."

"Sorry, it was the champagne."

That will teach me to serve Roederer to a street urchin, I thought, as we headed toward the Vavin Métro station, where we would go our separate ways. Pétronille must have sensed that the incident had put me off a bit, because she didn't say "see you soon."

Alone again, I took myself to task. Was it really so terrible to pee between two parked cars? Why was I acting as if I'd been traumatized? To be sure, no one in Japan would ever behave like that. But that was precisely why I had left the Land of the Rising Sun to come to France, because I appreciated the sense of freedom here. "You're just an old fussbudget," I thought.

The fact remains that I did not get back in touch with Pétronille. The years went by and I gave no further thought to my search for a drinking companion. That was my way of remaining loyal to my acquaintance of an evening.

October, 2001. I was browsing through the new books in a Paris bookstore when I came upon *Honey Vinegar,* a first novel by one Pétronille Fanto.

I gave a start and grabbed the book. On the back cover was written: "An insolent debut novel by Pétronille Fanto, 26, a specialist in Elizabethan literature." There was a little black-and-white author photograph: she hadn't changed. I smiled, and bought the book.

I have a very particular protocol when reading. I have learned that to ensure the highest degree of absorption, I must read lying down, preferably on a soft cozy bed: the farther I vanish from any physical self-awareness, the better I merge with the text. And so it was in this case.

I read *Honey Vinegar* in one sitting. Pétronille—the nerve of it!—had revived the theme of Montherlant's *The Girls*: a bestselling author receives letters from female readers who have fallen in love with him, and replies with a mixture of voracity and weariness. The similarity went no further, for while Montherlant's Costals emerges victorious from the confrontation, Fanto's Schwerin is thoroughly devoured by the maidens.

Montherlant, from the height of his long career as a bestselling author, wrote from experience. Pétronille, on the other hand, had launched into her topic as a debut novelist. What could she possibly know about the behavior of female readers? But this paradox would have been totally uninteresting were it not for her talent: not only was she bold, she also—and above all—showed real mastery where language and narration were concerned.

Better still: it was clear that she had an exemplary assimilation of culture. Here was an author who had read everything, and not just recently; she was well beyond the stage where one might feel the need to flaunt one's knowledge in front of others. Proof of this, the debt she owed Montherlant seemed so obvious to her that she made no reference to him whatsoever—and this in an era where young people her age hardly read him at all anymore.

Such supreme elegance is bound to disappear. Four or five years ago, a reader in her twenties wrote and accused me of plagiarism. Derisively, my sly reader explained what she had found: according to her, one sentence in my novel *Hygiene and the Assassin* had been lifted word for word from *Cyrano de Bergerac*: "I may use them on myself with a witty turn of phrase, but I will not allow other people to use them." "And you did not reference it…" she concluded, with an accusatory ellipsis. More fool I, I answered the young woman and confidently expressed my belief that half the planet must know where the quotation came from. She immediately wrote back to inform me that she was the only student in her year in liberal arts who recognized the quote, hence my defense was unconvincing. Which just goes to show that in this day and age a desire to eschew priggish pedantry is tantamount to premeditated theft.

Her youth notwithstanding, Pétronille had earned her

position among the ranks of congenial authors. I was glad of this, and I immediately penned an enthusiastic letter, which I sent to her through her publisher's good offices. I soon received a reply inviting me to a signing. On the designated date and time I made my way to a cozy bookstore in the twentieth arrondissement called Le Merle Moqueur.

I absolutely love to go to other authors' book signings. For once I don't have to do the work. Moreover, I love to watch how my colleagues go about it. There are some who are rude and hardly look at the reader while they are signing, or who keep their cell phone wedged between ear and shoulder and refuse to interrupt their telephone conversation. There are some who get it over with quickly, and then others who are even slower than I am—I recall one adorable Chinese fellow who was the despair of all the booksellers because he spent half an hour with each reader, first thinking, then "signing" the calligraphic inscription each reader inspired in him. Some authors go too far, or behave obsequiously, not to mention the ones who chat up the women. It's endlessly entertaining.

In Pétronille's case, the most notable thing was the attitude of the readers. They all stared at her with disbelief when they saw that she was the author. Like four years ago, she resembled a fifteen-year old boy. Such a juvenile air made her debut novel all the more improbable.

Her manner with people was one of frank courtesy—the best. I recalled how she had peed on the sidewalk of the rue Huyghens and now I saw the event differently: no doubt Christopher Marlowe and Ben Jonson would have done the same. And what could be more chic than the manners of Shakespeare's contemporaries? Pétronille actually did have something roguish about her, which she would have shared with those great authors, many of whom died before the age of thirty in senseless tavern-leaving brawls. How much classier could you get?

When it was my turn, she said, "Amélie Nothomb at my book signing: all right!"

I handed her *Honey Vinegar.*

"A real treat," I said.

"So did you bring the champagne?"

"I'm sorry, I didn't think."

"Pity. I've got a Pavlovian reflex with you now: every time I see you I develop the most incredible craving for Roederer."

"Let me take you out afterwards. We'll find some Roederer."

"If it's only Veuve or Dom, I won't turn my nose up at it."

"Laurent-Perrier, Moët, Taittinger, Krug, Philipponnat," I recited, at the speed of a straight flush.

"Fine," she said soberly.

While she was finishing up, I read what she had written on the flyleaf: "To Amélie Nothomb, patron of the arts." And then her signature.

She said goodbye to the bookseller and then we were out on a street in the twentieth arrondissement.

"If I've understood you correctly, my patronage consists in plying the artists I admire with alcohol?" I asked.

"Exactly. Well, you could even go so far as to invite them to dinner."

I took her to the Café Beaubourg, where I was a regular. I apprised Pétronille of the fact that the establishment did have toilets.

"You can be so old hat!" she said.

We spent a very pleasant evening. Pétronille filled me in

about the last four years. She had been earning her living as a supervisor in a private lycée while she worked on her novel. A big kid in the final year had called her a "pleb"; she answered back that he was a "toff." The poor little boy went whining to his parents, who demanded that the subordinate apologize to the dear angel. Pétronille countered that "toff" was no more of an insult than "pleb," and that was a fact, so there was no reason to be offended. The headmistress dismissed Pétronille.

"One week later I found a publisher for *Honey Vinegar*," she concluded.

"Excellent timing."

"It's going well. Don't hesitate to invite me to some of your fancy parties, I'm not very well known in the circles you frequent."

"I think you might be getting the wrong idea about the kind of life I lead."

"Go on, you're young and famous, you must get invited everywhere."

"Young? I'm thirty-four."

"Well, then you're old and famous."

It was true that I received invitations to everything, but I always declined them. It occurred to me then that perhaps these society events would not be so boring in the company of Pétronille.

"I have an invitation to an afternoon of champagne tasting at the Ritz at the end of the month."

"You're on."

I smiled. My initial scheme had been to make her my drinking companion. And it seemed to be falling into place, effortlessly.

On the appointed day Pétronille was waiting for me outside the Ritz. As usual she was wearing jeans and a leather jacket, and Doc Martens. As for me, I was dressed like a turn of the century Templar.

"I look like a hooligan compared to you," she said.

"You're fine."

The salons of the Ritz were infested with society matrons who inspected my friend from head to toe with open disgust. Such a lack of refinement unsettled me, and I cringed.

"Do you want us to leave?" she asked.

"Out of the question."

We had come for the champagne, after all. There were several tables, with different brands. We started with a Perrier-Jouët. A wine steward recited a promising little spiel. In such instances I love being the converted to whom one preaches.

Champagne almost tastes better at these society gatherings. The more hostile the context, the more the drink acts as an oasis, something you cannot get from tippling at home.

The first flute was delightful.

"Not bad stuff," said Pétronille to the wine steward.

The man gave her a kindly smile. All the wine stewards I have met are exquisite creatures, without exception. I don't know if it is the profession that makes them that way or if it is their choice of métier that presupposes it. That day, at the Ritz, the wine stewards were the only ones worth the time of day.

As we moved around the room, I was immediately harpooned by ladies who gushed that they had seen me on television. That was all they had to say, but it took forever. I interrupted:

"Allow me to introduce Pétronille Fanto, a talented young novelist."

Every time, these creatures in their headbands were petrified. Their expression veered from ecstatic where I was concerned to disdainful with regard to the guttersnipe I was hoping to introduce. Suddenly they had a mission of the utmost importance elsewhere. Pétronille, forthright, would hold out her hand, and many of them had the effrontery not to shake it.

"Do I smell like dog food?" she asked, with disgusted disbelief, which I shared.

"I do apologize," I said. "I didn't expect such bold-faced rudeness."

"It's not your fault. Really, I'm glad to be here. You have to see it to believe it."

"The champagne won't snub you, that's for sure. Let's go try the Jean-Josselin."

It turned out to be excellent. To the best of my knowledge it is the only champagne that tastes of yeast: a marvel.

As we had to be sure to avoid ladies with headbands and concentrate on the tasting, we ended up dead drunk. In company, I become joyful and expansive. As I could hardly share my agreeable disposition with the other guests at the gathering, I was ever so jolly with the wine stewards, and with Pétronille I turned confiding.

She was in an advanced state of inebriation, and quickly proved openly rebellious. She hardly listened to what I said, replying rather with sharp observations about the other guests. Our conversation took this sort of turn:

"I think one of the goals in life is to be plastered, at night, in a beautiful city."

"Where on earth did they find this bunch of shrews, anyway?"

"There are things to nibble on over at the buffet but I don't recommend them. My sister Juliette says, and she's right, that while wine improves food, the opposite is never true. The despicable race of connoisseurs scream with rage at the thought. And yet I have always found it to be true: take one bite and drinking loses its magical edge."

"If she goes on staring at me I am going to plant my foot in her ugly face."

"I have nothing against food, but I think you should only begin to dine when you can no longer take another sip. Which significantly delays the time you sit down to eat."

"But is she even worth me lifting my foot off the floor, I kinda doubt it."

"Sometimes I've delayed dinner so long that I couldn't eat. When that happens, it is sheer ecstasy simply to collapse from drunkenness onto a voluptuous sofa. You have to learn to plot carefully and well ahead of time the location for your collapse. The Ritz is not ideal. Henceforth I will make sure I only accept places that are conducive to divine subsidence."

"I'm going to ask her if she wants my picture."

Mechanically, I followed Pétronille, continuing to pour out my thoughts. I had no idea she was actually going to ask this woman if she wanted her photograph.

"I beg your pardon?" said the woman, practically choking.

"Just give me your address and I'll send it to you. I know just how you must feel: a picture of an authentic pleb, you can't get much more exotic than that."

Terrified, the woman gave me an imploring look, as if begging for help. I merely performed my socially appointed role: "Dear Madam, allow me to introduce Pétronille Fanto, a young novelist whom I admire. Her debut novel, *Honey Vinegar,* is bursting with talent."

"How very interesting! I shall buy it," said the lady, trembling.

"Great idea, my photo is on the back cover. That way you can stare at me to your heart's content."

What a sublime conclusion. I grabbed Pétronille by the arm. I could tell that if I didn't restrain her, she would vent her spite unremittingly.

We tried yet another champagne. At this point, I would be lying if I claimed to remember what it was. But it was delicious and graciously served. Pétronille no longer pretended to be tasting: instead of taking a sip with a contemplative air to appreciate the bouquet, she now gulped down the entire contents of the flute in one go and then held it out to the wine steward and said, "Tide's out!"

The gentleman filled it up for her again with a charming smile. Intuitively, I did not trust his good manners. If things went on like this, Pétronille would ask to drink straight out of the bottle, and the man would hand it to her as if it were the most natural thing on earth.

"It's getting a bit stuffy in here," I said in a hushed voice. "I think it's time to go."

Grave mistake. Pétronille exclaimed, very loudly, "You think it's stuffy in here? I don't. It's just warming up, don't you think?"

Everyone turned to look at us. My cheeks on fire, I tried to coax my friend over to the door. An endeavor that was harder than I anticipated. She went all heavy and floppy, and I couldn't simply lead her by the hand. In the end I had to shove her forward as if she were a piece of furniture.

"But I haven't tried all the champagnes!" she protested.

Outside the Ritz, the fresh air took a slight edge off our inebriation. I sighed with relief, and Pétronille vociferated: "I was having a good time in there!"

"As for me, when I'm drunk I love to walk around the posh neighborhoods in Paris."

"You call this posh?" she roared, scornfully considering the Place Vendôme.

"So show me the part of Paris you love," I answered.

She liked the idea. She took me by the arm and led me toward the Tuileries, then the Louvre (she pointed to it and confessed, "Now it really is not bad, after all.") We crossed the Pont du Carrousel ("As rivers go, the Seine is the very best," she declared) and went the length of the quais at a brisk clip. We went past the Place Saint-Michel and ended up outside a bookshop worthy of a novel by Dickens: the sign read "Shakespeare and Company."

"Here we are," she said.

I had never heard of this fairy-tale place. Enchanted, I gazed at both the outside and the inside: through the window you could see books that looked as if they must be full of magic spells, and booklovers whom no one disturbed in their reading, and a young blond bookseller, her skin like porcelain, so pretty and gracious that just to look at her you knew you had to be dreaming.

"Shakespeare really is your patron saint," I concluded.

"Find me a better one."

"That would be impossible. But what you love about Paris is not all that Parisian."

"That's open to debate. Even in Stratford-upon-Avon you won't find anything like this bookstore. But having said that, if it's ultra-Parisian you want, then follow me."

We went deeper into the narrow streets of the fifth arrondissement. She made her way, as surefooted as a Sherpa. I eventually realized where she was taking me.

"The Arènes de Lutèce!" I exclaimed.

"I love this place. It's so anachronistic. In Rome a site like this would seem so ordinary that no one would notice. But in Paris, where all the Antiquity is underground, it's a real treat to have a relic of the era when we were Lutetians."

"Speak for yourself. I'm from Belgic Gaul. The only country in the world whose name—in French anyway—comes from an adjective turned into a noun."

We gazed respectfully at the arena. A silence of catacombs reigned.

"I feel very Gallo-Roman," declared Pétronille.

"Tonight, or in general?"

"You are so not normal," she answered with a laugh.

I didn't understand, so I disregarded her remark.

"Actually, Pétronille is the feminine for Petronius," I continued. "As in Petronius Arbiter—you are a little arbiter of elegance."

"Why little?"

You were not supposed to joke about the fact she was only five foot three.

A prestigious women's magazine offered me a commission to go to London and interview Vivienne Westwood.

I hadn't been accepting commissions for quite some time. But in this case I yielded to temptation for two reasons: first of all, in order to step on English soil at last—however strange it might seem, even by 2001 I had never been there—and the second, obviously, to meet the extraordinary Vivienne Westwood, an icon as chic as she is punk. It didn't help matters that my contact at the magazine was an exquisite woman who described the mission to me in the following terms:

"Madame Westwood was brimming with enthusiasm when I said your name. She described your style as being deliciously continental. I think she'd be thrilled to treat you to a garment from her new collection."

I capitulated. The journalist graciously expressed her delight. A room would be booked at a luxury hotel. A car would come and fetch me, etc. As she spoke, I began to see the film she was describing. And I wanted everything in that film, avidly.

It made sense. The Nothomb family is of distant English extraction. They left Northumberland in the eleventh century and crossed the Channel, just to be contrary to

William the Conqueror. If I had waited this long to visit the island of my forebears, it was because I needed this nod from fate: the grunge-queen of crinolines, holding out her hand, "brimming with enthusiasm" (besotted, I said the journalist's words to myself over and over).

So, in December 2001, I boarded the Eurostar for the very first time. When the train went down into the famous tunnel, my heart began to pound. Over my head was this significant body of water my ancestors had seen fit to cross in the other direction one millennium earlier. In the event of a loss of watertightness, the Eurostar would be transformed into a underwater missile, to streak through the fish all the way to the famous cliffs. I found my fantasy so beautiful that I was beginning to wish it would come true, when the train burst into a desolate winter landscape.

I let out a cry. I gazed, stunned, at this unfamiliar countryside. Before we crossed the Channel, the empty fields had been dreary too, but now, I felt the nature of their dreariness was different. This was English sadness. The streets, the signs, the few dwellings I could see—everything was different.

Later, I saw on my left an immense redbrick industrial ruin that took my breath away. I never found out what it was.

When the train pulled into Waterloo Station, I almost wept for joy. As I stepped out onto British soil at last, I felt like the queen of the ball. I was sure the earth trembled as it recognized the footstep of its distant progeny. A taxi drove me to the hotel, as promised, and it met my every expectation: I had a room as vast as a cricket field; the size of the bed provided ample sparring room for a billionaire couple negotiating a divorce.

I like to travel light and consequently I was already wearing the appropriate clothing: since this was how Vivienne Westwood had described me, I had put on the most continental of my lace redingotes and my Belgian Diabolo hat. I made my complexion snowy white, my eyes charcoal black, and my lips carmine red. Outside the lobby, a car was waiting for me.

When I arrived at the legendary boutique, I was not made to use the front entrance, but rather a porte cochère around the back, which led directly to the workshop. Enchanted, I craned my neck to attend to the miracle of creation, but not a minute later I was ushered into a tiny storage room furnished with two benches and smelling of rubber tires.

"Miss Westwood shall arrive soon," said the man in black who had taken me there.

There were no windows in the room, and as I waited I began to feel anxious. After ten minutes or so the man in black opened the door and said, "Miss Westwood."

Into the room came a lady with long carrot-purée-colored hair. She held out a limp hand, neither looking at me nor speaking, then she collapsed on a bench, without inviting me to sit down. I nevertheless sat on the other bench and told her how delighted I was to meet her.

I got the impression that my words had fallen into a black hole.

Vivienne Westwood had just turned sixty. In 2001 no one thought of this as old anymore. I would gladly have made an exception in her case. It was all about her tight-lipped expression, the surly slant to her mouth, and above all her resemblance to the ghost of the aging Queen Elizabeth I: the same faded ginger coloring, the same coldness, the same conviction that one was dealing with someone ageless. She was wearing a straight skirt in a golden tweed and a sort of bodice over the skirt, in the same hue. Such eccentricity in no way attenuated her bourgeois demeanor. It was hard to believe that there could ever have been any connection between a punk aesthetic and this tubby biddy.

I had met many unpleasant people in my life, but none of them compared to this massive wall of scorn. At first I thought she didn't understand my English because of my accent; as I expressed this concern, she murmured, "I've managed to understand worse than you."

Discountenanced, I went ahead with the questions I had planned. It is infinitely more difficult to ask questions than to answer. At her age, Vivienne Westwood must have been well aware of this fact. However, every time I had the audacity to interrogate her, she gave a little sigh, or even stifled a yawn. Then she would come out with a generous answer, which went to show that she was not displeased with my question.

The commissioning journalist had told me that, on hearing my name, "Miss Westwood brimmed with enthusiasm." How well she hid it! This must be what they meant by "stiff upper lip."

"May I visit the workshop?" I asked.

What had I said? Vivienne Westwood looked at me with indignant wrath. She did not deign to answer, and I was grateful to her for that, for no doubt she would have raked me over the coals.

So unsettled that I no longer knew what to say, I asked, on the off-chance, "Miss Westwood, have you ever wanted to write?"

A pinnacle of scorn, she spluttered, "Write?! Please, don't be vulgar. There is nothing more vulgar than writing. Nowadays the most insignificant football player writes. No, I do not write. I leave that to others."

Did she know whom she was talking to? I began to hope that she did not. It would be better to be a complete unknown where this woman was concerned than to subject oneself to such an affront.

I behaved the way a Japanese woman would: I laughed. It seemed to me that I'd touched bottom. Even if it brings bad luck to think like that. Reality always rushes in to prove how greatly you lack imagination.

I heard a strange scratching noise coming from the other side of the door. With her chin, Vivienne Westwood motioned to me to open the door. I did as she asked. In bounded a black poodle, trimmed according to the latest fashion, and it trotted over to the designer. Her expression changed in the most extraordinary way. Her face filled with tenderness and she cried out, "Beatrice! Oh, my darling!"

She took the dog in her arms and covered it with kisses. Her face was streaming with love.

I was enthralled. *A person who loves animals this much cannot be all bad*, I thought.

Beatrice began yapping in a way that probably meant to say something, but I could not tell what. Miss Westwood must have understood the significance of the dog's behavior, because she put her down and said, curtly, "It is time to walk Beatrice."

I nodded: when Beatrice started yapping, it meant that nature was calling.

"It is time to walk Beatrice," she said again, petulantly.

I looked at the man in black, who was standing on the other side of the door, which had remained open: had he not heard the order addressed to him?

"Don't you understand English?" she eventually said to me, wearily.

At last I understood. It was to me, and me alone, that she was communicating what was not a request but an order.

I asked her for the leash. She took some sort of S&M accessory out of her bag and handed it to me. I fastened it to Beatrice's collar and left the room. The man in black indicated the route to follow. Which wasn't indispensable, because the dog knew the way.

Beatrice led me to a square where she was used to going. I tried to grasp the poetry of the moment: was this not a singular way to discover London? But no matter how I tried to view the episode as positively as I could, there was nevertheless a feeling of shame that floated on the surface. I dared to examine it more closely: first Vivienne Westwood had insulted me, then she had ordered me to walk her dog. Yes, that was exactly what had happened.

I looked around me. The square seemed as ugly as all the buildings surrounding it. People had horrible expressions on their faces. Finally, the damp chill went right to the bone. I had to face facts: I did not like London at all.

Lost in my feelings of disgust, I had forgotten about the canine race and her majesty Beatrice, who was yapping and hopping, showing me the poop she had just produced. I wondered if English law required one to remove the turd; given my ignorance thereof, I decided not to touch it. If a policeman stopped me, I would give him the contact information for the boutique.

For a split second a devilish flash of inspiration told me to kidnap the poodle and demand a ransom. As if to dissuade me, Beatrice began biting my calves in exasperation. It is absolutely true what people say, that dogs resemble their masters. I went back. Vivienne Westwood gave Beatrice to the man in black and then asked me: Had the little creature taken communion of both kinds? How was the poop? This was the only time she listened scrupulously to what I had to say. After that, she relapsed into her scorn and ennui.

As I did not see any point in prolonging the ordeal I took my leave. Miss Westwood held out a limp hand without looking at me any more than upon greeting me, and she returned to the job at hand. I was out in the street, prey to an acute awareness of how far I had fallen.

In short: I had just been treated, literally, worse than a dog, by an aging punkette disguised as Queen Elizabeth I—unless it was the other way around—in a metropolis where I knew nothing and no one. Now I was all alone on an inhospitable street, and a freezing cold drizzle was beginning to fall. In a stupor, I began to walk in what I believed was the direction of my hotel. If I had had one iota of common sense, I would have taken a taxi, but Londoners now filled me with a sort of terror, even those behind the wheel of a car, and I preferred to have nothing more to do with that strange species.

Under normal circumstances I enjoy getting lost in strange cities, and I profess that there is no better initiation to a place. But that is not what I felt that day. Huddling for shelter under a tiny rickety umbrella, I wandered down absurd avenues lined on either side with edifices whose windows gazed out at me with Vivienne Westwood's expression. All I could feel was a hateful chill, and I recalled the words of Victor Hugo: "London is boredom constructed." His concise formula was still too positive, in my opinion. If the rest of England was anything like the capital, I could understand why people referred to the country as perfidious Albion, and I felt boundless empathy with my ancestors who had fled Northumberland a thousand years earlier. Every building I went by seemed to emanate something insidiously hostile.

Eventually I had to ask my way from some natives who pretended not to understand my English, and I refrained from telling them that even their glorious old fashion designer could understand my mumbo-jumbo. After two hours of desperate drifting, I reached the hotel, where I locked myself in my room to keep the enemy at bay. I marinated for a long time in a steaming bath, then I climbed into bed. All too quickly, my appreciation for such comfort gave way to an unpleasant concession of failure. Never in my life had I so failed to appreciate a city. If it had been Maubeuge or Vierzon I might have laughed about it. But London, honestly!

London, where Shakespeare had written and staged his greatest masterpieces, where European honor had been saved during the last war, where all sorts of avant-garde movements were flourishing. I was the one who was being punished for having failed to appreciate the city. To be sure, Vivienne Westwood was a blow dealt by fate, but it was totally unfair on my part to blame the entire city! Was I really, at the age of thirty-four, about to order a club sandwich from room service and bolt myself in my room, despite the fact that this was my first night in England?

Instinctively I reached for the telephone.

"Hello, Pétronille. Would you like to come and spend the evening with me?"

"Sure, why not?"

"I'm in London."

"Oh, I see. Well, that changes things."

"I'll give you the money for the train. If you don't mind, you can share my suite, which is as big as Buckingham Palace."

I gave her the address of the hotel.

"I'm on my way."

At nine o'clock there was a knock on my door. To see a friendly face there before me on that hostile shore filled me with joy. I began pouring my heart out, but she interrupted me:

"I'm hungry. Let's go have dinner. You'll tell me your story on the way."

I followed her through the dark streets, describing my calamitous encounter with Vivienne Westwood. Pétronille laughed wholeheartedly.

"You think it's funny?"

"Yes. I suppose it wasn't so funny in reality. The business with the poodle!"

"What would you have done in my shoes?"

"I would have gotten out my repertory of Scottish insults and flung them at the old cow."

"That's my problem. I don't know any Scottish insults."

"Go on. Even if you had known a few, you wouldn't have said anything. I read your book, *Fear and Trembling.*"

She was right. Coarse behavior in others has no effect on me, other than to petrify me. In the meantime, we were standing outside a greasy spoon that gave off enticing odors.

"What do you say to some Indian food? Unless you really want a meat pie."

In no time their excellent food had cheered me up. Then Pétronille took me to a pub where she ordered two pints of Guinness straight off. A pioneering rock band was playing some weird music they called "dubstep."

"You mustn't drink the foam on its own," said Pétronille when she saw me lapping it up. "Guinness is good when you drink it through the foam. Not to mention the fact that you look idiotic when you lap up the foam."

"I like this music. It sounds as if they're putting the bass through a curling iron."

"And to think that if I hadn't come you wouldn't have left the hotel room."

"I was traumatized. I thought you were the only one who might give me the nerve to go out."

"Stop making such a fuss, you've seen worse—all that for a bigheaded harpy."

Late that night, Pétronille led me to a narrow street of the more cutthroat variety. She stood in a very particular place and said, extremely solemnly, "There. I am standing in the exact spot where Christopher Marlowe was murdered."

I was surprised to feel a shiver go through me.

"You bear a frightening resemblance to Christopher Marlowe," I said.

"You have no idea what he looked like," she shot back.

"No, indeed I don't. But your bad-boy side does give you some striking similarities to Shakespeare's contemporaries."

"The things you come out with sometimes!"

Later, I had the opportunity to see a portrait of Christopher Marlowe. My intuition proved correct: there was a strange resemblance to Pétronille. If you shaved off

Marlowe's goatee and mustache, you would get Pétronille, with her chubby face and her juvenile, mischievous air.

It must have been one o'clock in the morning when we went back to the hotel room. When I woke up three hours later to write, I saw that Pétronille was asleep on the far side of the colossal bed. It looked as if she hadn't gotten undressed.

I went into the living room of the suite to write, refusing to let the Victorian furnishings intimidate me. As on every other day of my life, the phenomenon kept me in its grip for roughly four hours, then deserted me. Through the window I saw what must have been the equivalent of a sunrise on this side of the Channel: a slight attenuation of the darkness.

Pétronille had never seen me in my writing outfit (a pair of what you might describe as Japanese antinuclear pajamas) and I was determined not to traumatize her. I was tiptoeing through the bedroom toward the bathroom when I heard, "What on earth is that?"

"It's me."

A silence, followed by, "Right. It's worse than I thought."

"I'll get changed, if you want."

"No, no. If I turn on the light, will it catch fire?"

"Go right ahead."

She switched on the light and looked at me once again.

"Oh, it was worth the trip just for the color. How would you describe it?"

"*Kaki.*"

"No. Khaki is green and you're dark orange."

"Yes, the color of the *kaki*, the Japanese persimmon fruit. This is my writing outfit."

"And does it yield good results?"

"I'll let you be the judge of that."

She laughed and got up. It was my turn to be surprised.

"You didn't get undressed before going to bed, not even your shoes!"

"I'm a real cowboy. That way, if someone attacks us in the night, I'm ready."

"Are you serious?"

"No, I was exhausted."

"I'll order breakfast. What would you like?"

"Anything but their bloody sausages, porridge, and kidneys. Coffee, toast, and jam."

While I was calling room service, she went to take a shower. Breakfast was served in the dining room. Like my Lord and Lady, we sat at either end of a very long table.

"This is really practical for passing the sugar," said Pétronille.

"I like it."

"Have you seen how unflappable these people are? The breakfast lady didn't bat an eyelash when you opened the door in your orange pajamas."

"I'm sure she's seen worse in her life."

"I haven't."

I burst out laughing.

"What do you want to do this morning?"

"What seems interesting to you, here?" I asked.

"Well, the fact the museums are free, that's good, isn't it?"

"Indisputably."

"Let's go to the British Museum."

Which is what we did. Not to lose each other, we arranged to meet in Mesopotamia at noon. It's not every day you can schedule a meeting in such a place.

When I am in an edifice like this, I appreciate the ensemble even more than the details. I like to wander around, but I obey no other logic than my own pleasure, from ancient Egypt to Galapagos by way of Sumer. To stuff myself with the entirety of Assyriology would leave me nauseated, whereas nibbling a few cuneiform characters as an aperitif, some runes for the starter, the Rosetta stone for the main course and a few prehistoric negative hand prints for dessert really fires up my taste buds.

What I cannot abide in museums is the ponderous pace people feel duty-bound to respect. I am the sort who goes through at a brisk pace, incorporating whole vast prospects with my gaze: whether it is archaeology or Impressionist painting, I have tested the advantages of my method. The first is that I am spared the atrocious "guidebook effect": "Admire the good-natured aspect of Sheikh al-Balad: don't you feel you met him at the market only yesterday?" Or: "Litigation is opposing Greece and the United Kingdom over the Elgin marbles." The second advantage is concomitant with the first: it makes it impossible to chat about what you've seen on leaving the museum. Any modern-day Bouvard and Pécuchet would have the wind taken right out of their sails. The third advantage, and not the least important as far as I'm concerned, is that a brisk pace prevents the onset of the dreaded museum backache.

At around noon I realized that I was lost. I went up to a museum official and said:

"Mesopotamia, please."

"Third floor, and turn left," he answered as simply as could be.

Which just goes to show that you would be wrong to

think that Mesopotamia is so inaccessible. True to our arrangement, Pétronille was there waiting for me. I appreciated the fact that she spared me a digested version of her tour. Instead, she suggested we go for fish and chips.

"Really?" I asked.

"Yes. It's something you have to try when you're in the UK. Well worth it. I know a good place in Soho."

In the designated hole in the wall, she wasted no time in splattering my plate with a generous amount of vinegar. Thanks to which I had to concede it was very tasty.

"Shall we say *tu* to each other?" she suggested, taking a sip of beer.

"Why should we?"

"We've slept in the same bed, I've seen you in your orange pajamas, and now we're eating fish and chips together. It seems strange to go on saying *vous*."

"For me, the only question is this: what would we gain by saying *tu*?"

"Never mind, you're against it."

"Ten times out of ten, I must confess."

"It's your upbringing."

"On the contrary. In my family, we say *tu* as often as possible. No, it's visceral: I like saying *vous* to people."

"I see."

"Wait, there are two of us here."

"Which voids the vote altogether: one for, one against."

"Yes. But why should my vote be the one to carry it? That's not fair."

"Well, we're not about to toss a coin, are we?"

"Yes, that's exactly what we'll do. Chance is a form of justice worthy of the name."

Pétronille took a penny from her pocket and said, "Heads, it's *vous*, tails it's *tu*."

She flicked the coin into the air with her thumb. Never had I so fervently hoped to see the Queen's face.

"Tails!" she cried.

"This will be tough."

"Just say the word and we'll keep using *vous.*"

"No, no. I'll get it wrong a lot of the time, but I'll get there eventually."

After lunch, we walked past a vintage boutique selling secondhand Doc Martens. I saw some royal blue ones, with straps, in fairly good condition. Pétronille decreed that they suited me to a T.

"They'll make a nice change from your loony bin standard issue."

"And why do my shoes deserve so much sarcasm?"

"If you were normal, you would understand."

"You see that saying *tu* to me is not without consequence. Look at how you're suddenly referring to me."

"It's not sudden. Last night I called you idiotic."

My serenity absurdly restored, I bought the Doc Martens with the straps. I still wear them, to this day.

On our way to the station we passed an individual walking a corgi. We both went into raptures.

"I am crazy about those dogs!" cried Pétronille.

"Me too. They're my favorite dog. And the Queen's, as well."

"Now that you mention it, you look like a cross between a corgi and Queen Elizabeth II. Half and half."

She wouldn't give up.

On the Eurostar, Pétronille asked me for my verdict about London.

"Until you got there, I thought it was purgatory."

"And once I got there?"

"Hellacious."

She let out a boisterous laugh.

"You're right, we had a good time."

It is true that thanks to her, I did get something out of my lightning visit. Nevertheless, when we got to the Gare du Nord, and I found myself in that neighborhood that is hardly what you'd call charming, I suddenly understood why people say "gay Paree":

"What a joyful, lighthearted city!"

"Shall we go drink some champagne?" suggested Pétronille.

She was right, the two went together. At the first bistro we found, opposite the station, I ordered a bottle of Taittinger. As we drank, we gave vent to all our anti-English sentiment: what better way to create an atmosphere? When it came time to go our separate ways, we had to admit that we did not believe a word of what we had said.

When I got home I immediately wrote my article, "An Interview with Vivienne Westwood," where I praised the woman to the skies. Nevertheless, I did not leave out any of the discourtesies she had heaped upon me, including the task of walking her poodle. When the commissioning editor received my article, she called me to offer her apologies.

"It's not your fault," I said. "What I don't understand is why you insisted that she was looking forward to meeting me."

"That's what her agent told me. And it would have been the least she could have done. What can I do to make it up to you? The psychological trauma you suffered…"

"You needn't go so far as to speak of psychological trauma. Why not summon the psychological support unit while you're at it?"

"No, you're right. But a few bottles of champagne, that ought to work wonders for psychological trauma."

This journalist obviously knew me well.

"Oh, you were talking about that type of psychological trauma. Well, what can I say, a few bottles of Laurent-Perrier..."

"Cuvée Grand Siècle?"

"You're right, we mustn't underestimate the psychological trauma I suffered."

The next day, four bottles of Laurent-Perrier Cuvée Grand Siècle were delivered to my door. At that rate, I'll gladly interview the nastiest old swine on the planet, and walk their poodles wherever they like.

In 2002 a second novel by Pétronille Fanto, *The Neon Light,* was published by Éditions Stock.

I rushed out to get it. The story was about contemporary adolescence. The hero, Léon, was a sort of fifteen-year-old Oblomov, dragging his entire family down in a nihilistic spiral. The book fascinated me even more than the first one had. In a subtle and comic way, it advocated despair.

I wrote to Pétronille, a letter of the sort only I can write. It is very difficult to express deep admiration to the person inspiring it. In person, that is the last thing I can do. But the pen provides me with a way to overcome the obstacle. In the shelter of the page, I can extricate myself from my excessive emotion. Pessoa has said that writing diminishes the fever of feeling. His sublime words do not apply to me; on the contrary: writing increases my feverish emotions, but the good thing about this worrying rise in an already critical temperature is that it allows clarity to emerge from the confusion in which I am steeped.

Pétronille called me. She seemed pleased with my letter, because she exclaimed, "Wow!"

"Thank you."

"Given your thoughts about my book, you must be

dying to invite me to drink some champagne. I have good news for you: I accept your invitation."

I had one bottle left from my post–Vivienne Westwood psychological compensation. At the end of the second flute I declared to Pétronille that in *The Neon Light* she was denouncing a current trend: the contamination of adults by adolescent values.

"What a pity you don't host a late-night panel show on France 2!" she said.

"Go ahead and laugh. It's true."

"We can continue this conversation at a bar, if that's where you're headed."

Pétronille liked to keep her conversation lighthearted, except when it was about politics. And there, sooner or later the daughter of the militant communist would show her face, and sooner or later she would exclaim—whether talking about salaries or unemployment or anything else: "You just don't realize how precarious this makes everything!"

This expression, which she still uses to this day when referring to the latest source of indignation, has always stunned me. I have never heard anyone other than Pétronille use it, not even politicians on the far left like Arlette Laguiller or Olivier Besancenot. For me, it is Pétronille's *hapax legomenon*. I have heard her apply it to things I could never have imagined would have the slightest rapport with being made precarious.

And that evening, when she informed me that she was going to be doing a signing in a prestigious Parisian bookstore, and I congratulated her, I saw her begin to fume with anger. I tried to get to the bottom of it. Out it came:

"Those bourgeois booksellers ought to be paying the

writers who come and waste two hours of their life signing books for them!"

"Now now, Pétronille, what are you on about? Booksellers already have a hard enough time as it is making ends meet. As far as a bookseller is concerned, they're taking a risk, inviting an author to sign at their store, but for the author, it's a gift!"

"You really buy all that, don't you? You're so naïve! I maintain that all work deserves a salary. To do a book signing without being paid puts you in a precarious situation."

I was speechless.

"Hey, the tide's gone out," she complained, handing me her empty champagne flute.

"We've drunk the entire bottle."

"So let's kill another one."

"No, I think we'll leave it there."

I had noticed that the more she drank the more she ventured into the far left of the left.

"What, only one bottle? You, Amélie Nothomb, with your apartment bubbling over with champagne? It's obscene! It's disgusting. It's…"

"Making things precarious?" I suggested.

"Exactly."

B eing Pétronille's drinking companion was not the most restful thing on earth. Not long thereafter, while she and I were sipping some Moët during God knows what literary event, she expressed an urge to go skiing. I don't remember exactly how the topic came up. I will resort to imagination and verisimilitude to reconstruct our conversation:

"Just look at these baboons. I swear, the more I hang around them, the greater my need for some fresh mountain air."

"I love the mountains," I said, innocently enough.

"Perfect. It's December. Before the month is out you and I will go skiing. Let's find someone."

I don't remember whom we contacted, but by the following morning we had a reservation for two people in an Alpine resort which for the sake of the story we shall call Dustin-les-Mites.

I called Pétronille to ask her how she had found it. Her inebriation was even more amnesiac than my own:

"Look, I don't remember a thing. But it will be fun, we're going skiing. Can you take care of the train tickets?"

She was right, after all. You have to force the hand of fate. If everything were left to my own initiative, nothing would ever happen in life.

On December 26 after two trains and a taxi we arrived in Dustin-les-Mites, at an altitude of 1200 meters. We dropped our things off at the chalet apartment. Pétronille was fidgeting with impatience. We had to put on our ski things at once and head for the front.

While we were waiting in line for tickets for the chair-lifts, she said, "When was the last time you went skiing?"

"In Japan."

"With that famous fiancé of yours, then?"

"No. When I was little."

Silence.

"How old were you?" she asked.

"Four."

"Are you telling me that you haven't been skiing since you were four years old?"

"I am."

"And now, how old are you?"

"Thirty-five."

Pétronille sighed with dismay.

"Don't count on me to give you lessons. I came here to have fun."

"I don't need your lessons."

"You haven't been skiing in over thirty years, Amélie!"

"I was a very good skier when I was four."

"Of course. You got your honorary snowflake at kindergarten. I'm impressed."

"It's like riding a bike, you don't forget."

"Of course you do."

"I believe in the genius of childhood."

Pétronille put her face in her hands and said, "We are headed for disaster."

"I promise you I can feel in my legs what I have to do."

At 2:30 we were on the slopes. The sun was shining, the snow conditions were perfect. My enthusiasm was at a peak.

Pétronille set off like a shot. In less time than it takes me to write this, she made her way down the vast slope, flowing with flawless elegance.

Cheerful as can be, I set off after her. Six feet farther along I fell flat on my face. I immediately got back on my feet and pushed myself forward, and a second later I was back on the ground. Fifteen times in a row I repeated the same rigmarole. Pétronille had time to take the T-bar and was now standing there next to me.

"The genius of childhood doesn't seem to be working. Do you want me to show you?"

"Leave me alone!"

Not even ten minutes later, she'd had time to go down and come back up, and was by my side as every five seconds I fell over.

"We have a problem," she said. "You're going to need a very patient instructor."

I burst into tears.

"And a psychiatrist," she added.

"Leave me alone! I'm sure I can do it! It's your presence that's stopping me. Can't you find some other slope—far, far away from this one?"

"All right."

She vanished.

So I was on my own, with two foreign bodies on my feet that were supposed to be a prolongation of my legs, but which so far had only made me feel like I had replaced my shoes with Ottoman sabers. I closed my eyes and went deep inside to look for my four-year-old self.

In the early 1970s, the Tyrol was all the rage where Japanese fantasies were concerned. My parents had rented a cuckoo clock of a chalet for a week, nestled in a resort in the Japanese Alps. The instructors wore lederhosen and the hostesses were in dirndls with bodices embroidered with edelweiss. It was Christmastime. Whenever we went to drink hot chocolate, there was always a Japanese choir singing in German, hymns to the glory of fir trees. To me it was a world of sublime strangeness.

On the slopes, the rudimentary instruction my mother gave me bore fruit. By the end of the week, I was like a flash of lightning on my tiny skis. I even knew how to turn.

"If I keep my eyes closed, I can do it," I decided now. And that is what I did: I thrust myself forward in total obscurity and, indeed, the feeling came back to me. By pivoting regularly, I made it to the bottom of the slope without falling over. I let out a cry of triumph.

As I was heading toward the T-bar, a string bean of a man skied up to me.

"What the hell are you doing? I was teaching my kids how to ski and you almost ran them down!"

"I'm sorry. It was because I had my eyes closed."

"Are you out of your mind?"

Perhaps I ought to change my method. Fortunately, once I got to the top of the slope, I discovered that even with my eyes open I could ski very well. What a delight to slalom through the powdery snow, and to use the bumps as ski jumps! What a marvelous sport! I tried some other slopes, and everything went my way. Pétronille caught up with me, flabbergasted.

"What happened?"

"I believe in the genius of childhood," I said again.

We skied in convoy until evening. How many times since that day have I heard Pétronille tell the story? "There I was on the ski slope with a beginner who was so useless she was in tears, and one hour later I found her zipping around like a pro! I swear, no way is this woman normal."

The next morning, Pétronille told me she'd had a very bad night's sleep. "This place is full of dust mites! I'm allergic."

"What can we do?"

"Open the windows."

We tried in vain to open the windows in the apartment. Clearly, we were not meant to open any of them. All our efforts were futile.

"This is crazy!" fumed Pétronille. "A closed-in space, with wall-to-wall carpeting, and we can't even air it out!"

"Isn't there anything else you can do about dust mites?"

"Vacuum cleaner."

In a closet I found a vacuum cleaner of the sort a slovenly bachelor might use: Pétronille eyed it scornfully. I went over the entire apartment. She shrugged.

"We should also shake out the comforters, and since we can't open the window…"

"That's no problem. I'll go shake them outside."

I seized each of the comforters bodily and went to shake them out in the street, mindless of people staring. Every time I went back in, Pétronille handed me something else to take down and shake out: pillows, sheets, bedspreads. I did my duty without flinching.

After my umpteenth trip, she informed me she would help me with the mattress.

"You won't be able to lift it by yourself."

"Wait a minute. We're going to shake the mattress out in the street?"

"Dust mites love to hide in mattresses. This mattress is a four-star hotel as far as they're concerned."

I didn't dare protest. Lifting the mattress, taking it down on our shoulders and getting it out into the fresh air was a veritable way of the cross. But that was nothing compared to the torture of shaking it out in the street and carrying it back up the narrow stairs.

Once we had managed to get it back into the apartment, Pétronille came out with, "Right. Your mattress, now."

"Why? I'm not allergic to dust mites!"

"Just think about it. There's one meter between our beds. For a dust mite, that is hardly what you'd call an insurmountable distance."

Resigned, I picked up my mattress and lugged it out into the street, thinking that Christ had been only a bit player, since he'd only had to walk his way of the cross once. Unless I'm Simon of Cyrene, I thought. And I laughed up my sleeve, imagining Christ turning to Simon the way Pétronille had turned to me: "Hey, are you gonna help me with this thing or not?"

We had not yet touched bottom. There in the street, while we were strenuously shaking the mattress, two policeman came up at a trot, alerted by some stalwart law-abiding neighbor.

"So, it's burglary in broad daylight now, is it?" said one of the officers.

"No, we're just cleaning house," I replied, breathlessly.

"Yeah, yeah. Your ID papers."

We had a great deal of difficulty in proving our innocence.

The hardest thing was to keep Pétronille from speaking, which I only managed to do by intervening with the humble and conciliatory tone the situation required. The policemen went away, saying, "Don't let us catch you at it again!"

Fortunately, they did not hear Pétronille's reply: "We'll be doing precisely that, first thing tomorrow morning!"

But I heard.

"Are you serious?"

"Of course! Dust mites die hard."

I was overcome by such deep discouragement that even when I was back on the slopes I did not enjoy myself at all: was it the prospect of having to move two mattresses every single day? All I felt was weariness and despondency.

At noon, Pétronille sighed: "I'm sick of skiing!"

"Already?"

"It's because of my bad night. Don't you have any ideas for how we can have more fun?"

I did have an idea. I left Pétronille to eat her croque-monsieur, and I hurried over to the minimarket. The only champagne they sold was Piper-Heidsieck. I came back with my rucksack weighed down with two bottles. When we reached the top of the slope on the T-bar, I informed my friend that I would stay there and she should come back to meet me there half an hour later. No sooner had she left than I buried the two bottles in the snow.

"What a marvelous region!" I thought. "No need for an ice bucket!" While I waited I spent my time imagining the number of grands crus I could chill in such a panorama. Japanese poetry got it right: it is the contemplation of landscapes that reveals us best.

Pétronille came back and declared that she was dead beat.

"I hope your surprise is a nice one."

I disinterred one of the champagne bottles. After opening her eyes wide, she made one of her typical comments: "I suppose you didn't think to bring any flutes."

Which is when I cleared the snow from the second bottle.

"That's why I bought two bottles. That way we each have our own."

"How elegant can you get!"

"The point is to drink while you're skiing. Skiing with a flute in your hand, that's James Bond stuff."

"Drink while skiing? You're crazy."

"No, just practical," I said. "Let's start down, what I mean is, let's start drinking here."

We uncorked the two bottles. When she had drunk half of hers, Pétronille decreed that it was worth trying to drink while skiing.

"The problem is we don't have three hands," she said.

"I've thought of that," I answered. "One pole in the right hand, and the bottle in the left."

"But we need the other pole!"

"I've seen one-armed skiers on disabled sports programs on television, and they manage fine."

I had done a damn good job preparing my argument. It was tailor-made to convince a lush who was hoping for nothing better.

The spare poles were fastened to my backpack and flatteringly replaced by a bottle of Piper-Heidsieck.

"Is this legal?" asked Pétronille.

"Something that has never been done is neither legal nor illegal," I said, decisively and firmly.

She set off first. I had never seen her ski so boldly. I slid onto the slope to follow her. The impression was extraordinary: it was as if the air and the snow were offering less resistance. Time had changed, too, and everything went by in a flash of ecstasy that seemed to last a thousand years.

"Bloody hell!" I exclaimed when I pulled up next to her. We each drank a deep draft of liquid gold.

"Yep," said Pétronille. "The problem is that it's impossible to refuel in flight."

"Maybe it's not entirely necessary."

"But hang on, we wanted to drink while skiing, no?"

"We're not obliged to attain absolute simultaneity. It's like coffee and cigarettes, they go well together, but you never have the smoke and the java in your mouth at the same time."

"Your comparison doesn't hold water."

"Drinking champagne means tilting your head back: and if you do that, you can't see the slope anymore. That's dangerous."

"Not if you drink fast."

"But that would be a pity!"

"So what, it's not Dom Pérignon, after all."

I stared at her, wide-eyed: I hadn't realized she was such a snob. She seized the moment to set off again. I stopped breathing when I saw her lift her elbow and tilt her head back in the midst of her slaloming. She lifted the bottle to her lips for a second which seemed to last an hour. "And to think that I'm the one who came up with this brilliant idea!" I moaned.

But there is a God watching over alcoholic skiers: she emerged unscathed. When she came to a halt, she looked at me and then raised her arms in a triumphant gesture.

My fear had sobered me; I caught up with her.

"Aren't you going to do like me?"

"No," I answered. "And I beg you, please don't repeat your exploit. I don't feel like having your death or anyone else's on my conscience."

"Go on, it's really because I'm such a nice girl."

I didn't reply. "Nice" is probably the least appropriate adjective there is on earth to describe her.

"What shall we do now?" grumbled Pétronille, pointing to her empty bottle.

"We'll keep on skiing until the intoxication fades."

"Fine. Which means we'll be back at the chalet five minutes from now."

We had to revise her forecast upwards: we kept on skiing until sunset. We laughed until we cried, took senseless risks (skiing up to bumps head-on, getting in the way of complete idiots who acted as if they were training for the Olympics), and made earth-shattering declarations ("People from Savoie are not really French!" cried Pétronille): in short, we had a smashing good time.

In the evening, in an excellent mood, we feasted on a muddled mixture of tartiflette, hot chocolate, toasted brioche, pickles, Ovomaltine energy bars, and raw onions.

"I think that even a rock concert of dust mites won't be able to keep me from sleeping," declared Pétronille, collapsing on her bed.

I did likewise and immediately fell into a heavy drunken sleep.

In the morning, looking distinctly green, she announced that she had not slept a wink.

"Dust mites die hard. I'm beginning to have trouble breathing."

She was wheezing asthmatically.

"Well, what will happen next?" I asked.

"It will only get worse."

"Right. I'm calling a taxi, we're going back to Paris."

"Wait a minute. Show me the booking contract for this shit week!"

I handed her the papers. She examined in great detail all the fine print that no one ever reads. One hour later she cried out, "I'm going to invoke this cancellation clause!"

She called the number printed in tiny characters and did not even need to pretend to speak in an asthmatic voice.

"People can die from an asthma attack, it's quite common," I heard her say.

When she hung up, she told me the ambulance was on its way.

"Are you going to the hospital?" I asked.

"No. We're going back to Paris, you and me. You're here to accompany me, it's legal."

"We're going back to Paris in an ambulance?"

"Yes," she said proudly. "Not only am I making it possible for you to save a large sum of money, but on top of it it'll be a lot faster. Get packing."

It was not long before we heard the ambulance siren. According to law, Pétronille had to board the ambulance on a stretcher. Which she was only too willing to do.

At first I thought she was acting, but once we were settled in the ambulance, with her lying down and me sitting next to her, I realized that she really was very sick. Here was someone who was even more asthmatic than I am.

It took six hours to go from Dustin-les-Mites to Paris. Pétronille gradually began to breathe more easily and regain some color. The ambulance crew were wonderful—competent and reassuring. When we reached the twentieth arrondissement in Paris, they asked her if she wanted to go home or to the hospital. She assured them she would feel better in her apartment.

I helped her carry her things up six flights of stairs without an elevator. Once she was settled in, she exclaimed, "No more winter sports, ever."

"It makes life too precarious?"

She ignored my question and declared, "We won't tell anyone we've come back, all right? I want to know what it feels like to be in Paris between the holidays when no one knows you're here."

"I know you're here."

"Yes. You have the right to look after me."

She viewed this as an authentic privilege. Since she was only just recovering from a very serious asthma attack, I treated her gently. I took her for slow walks in the gardens of the Châteaux of Versailles and Bagatelle, and in the Luxembourg Gardens. At the Salon de Thé Angelina we tasted the Mont Blanc and the hot chocolate. Such attentive behavior elicited the following expression of gratitude:

"You're a past master at dreaming up senior citizen activities."

"You're hardly choking on gratitude, are you."

On December 31, despite all my efforts via the telephone, I could not find a single restaurant with even a corner of a table available. So I suggested a New Year's Eve party with champagne and soft-boiled eggs at her place or mine. She did not seem very enthusiastic, then she said, "Why don't we go to my parents' place?"

"Are you serious?"

"Don't you want to?"

"I do! But I wouldn't want to bother them."

She shrugged, and called her parents.

"No problem," she said. "Unless you have a problem meeting people from the section."

"The section?"

"The Communist section from Antony."

The strangeness of the notion made me all the more eager to go. At the end of the afternoon Pétronille led the way to the RER B suburban train. In Antony we took a bus through a clean, depressing suburb. The Fanto parents lived in a little detached house her grandfather had built in the 1960s with his own hands. It was ordinary, and comfortable.

Pierre Fanto was a tall, friendly fellow in his fifties, and he introduced me to other guests from the section, a certain Dominique and a certain Marie-Rose. Marie-Rose was an old goat of the Stalinist school, as rigid as she was terrifying. Françoise Fanto, a slim, pretty woman, served the guests at the gathering with a shyness only I seemed to find surprising.

No matter what was said, it became apparent to me that the purpose was to obtain Marie-Rose's approval. I did not know whether she was higher ranking than the others, but she seemed to be the guardian of truth. For example, when Dominique dared to say that North Korea did not seem to be doing too well, she immediately broke in to say, "North Korea is doing much better than South Korea, and that's what matters."

Pierre described his recent trip to Berlin: he had come away concerned by the rise in prices. Marie-Rose did not let him go on:

"All the East Germans are aware of their lost happiness."

"Fortunately, we still have Cuba!" said Pierre.

I kept silent and observed Pétronille. But she was used to this and did not react; she stuffed her face with salami while her father put on some music. My lack of culture where French *chansonniers* were concerned was mindboggling, and I was naïve enough to ask who we were listening to.

"For Pete's sake, it's Jean Ferrat!" said Marie-Rose, indignantly.

Pierre opened an excellent bottle of Graves: finally a shared value. The wine relaxed the atmosphere.

"What's for dinner?" asked Pétronille.

"I've made my beef and carrot stew," answered her father.

"Ah, Pierre's beef and carrot stew!" said Dominique, ecstatic.

I was truly curious to taste this classic French dish, unknown in Belgium.

"You've never had beef and carrot stew?" said Pierre, astonished.

"So where are you from?" asked Marie-Rose.

"Belgium," I said cautiously, sensing that any more information than this would arouse her distrust.

They then embarked on a furious discussion of French politics. 2002 had been a disastrous year, and 2003 did not bode well. They commented on various changes in society that irritated them to the highest degree. Every time, Pierre would conclude angrily, "It's Mitterrand's fault!"

And the others agreed, loud and clear.

By midnight the discussion was still going strong. Françoise came in with a gorgeous *charlotte au chocolat* that she had made herself. I ate quite a hefty portion.

"These Belgians have a good appetite," said the section, approvingly.

I did not deny it. When the twelve fateful strokes rang out, we drank our champagne, a Baron Fuente.

"The only aristocrat you'll ever see in my house," said Pierre.

And the Baron held his own. In addition to its innumerable other benefits, champagne has the gift of cheering me up. And even if I don't know why I need cheering up, the drink definitely does.

At around two o'clock in the morning I collapsed on an old sofa and instantly fell asleep.

Several hours later, I was back on the RER heading to Paris with Pétronille.

"You all right? You weren't traumatized?" she asked.

"No. Why?"

"The section and their pronouncements."

"Reality far exceeded my wildest expectations."

She sighed: "I'm ashamed of my father."

"You shouldn't be. He's kind, and perfectly pleasant."

"Didn't you hear how he went on?"

"It hardly matters. His remarks may have been outrageous, but they were harmless."

"They haven't always been."

"Well they are now."

"All he does is rehash his father's opinions."

"You see, it's nothing more than filial allegiance. Reality isn't important to him."

"Exactly. And I suffered from it. For example: since

property is theft, he never locked the front door. And I don't know how many times we were burgled. It drove me crazy, I swear."

"I see. And what about your mother, does she share his opinions?"

"Who knows. She's as timid as she is intelligent. She's a party member but I think that in the polling booth she votes socialist."

"Is she afraid of your father? He doesn't look dangerous."

"She doesn't want to disappoint him. But she's not cut from the same cloth. What my mother really loves is opera. She's the one who chose my name."

"And your incredible literary culture, where did that come from?"

"It's a personal creation. My father only ever reads the communist press or books about the First World War, which is his passion. My mother reads things I would describe as 'entertaining.'"

"I see. You must have felt quite lonely!"

"You have no idea."

I stared out the window of the RER B at the suburban landscape. Objectively, you could do worse than these little houses, quiet streets and well-tended gardens. Then why did this panorama inspire such suicidal longings?

As we sped by I suddenly thought I could see, through the window of a dwelling, Pétronille's adolescence—the actual suffering of a little girl with absurdly aristocratic taste, who had embraced the ideals of the far left, but was at odds with the proletarian aesthetic—all those unabashedly ugly tchotchkes, and the shockingly stupid things they read.

I looked again at Pétronille. She was so much better than some cultured young lady. Her bad boy look, her fiery gaze, her nervous and muscular little body like that of a convict on the lam—and the strange softness of her face, which she shared with Christopher Marlowe. Like Marlowe, she could take as her motto: *Quod me nutrit, me destruit*: that which nourishes me destroys me. Great literature, which had gone to make up the bulk of her nourishment, was also what separated her from her loved ones, creating a gulf between them all the more impassable in that her tribe did not understand it.

Her parents loved her, and yet they were afraid of her. Françoise, who had a delicate soul, admired her daughter's novels and sometimes understood them. Pierre didn't understand a thing about them and couldn't see why her prose should outclass his personal diary.

I felt a powerful surge of admiration for Pétronille and I told her so.

"Thank you, bird," she replied.

Although I'd never made any overt references to birds in her presence, here she was decreeing that I belonged to the avian species. Her instinctive choice of words was spot-on: since the age of eleven, I have been obsessed with the winged race to the point of no return. I have spent so much time observing birds that I must have been infected by certain aspects of this animal kingdom. But what, exactly? I doubt whether language can help express it.

Some might say that the age of eleven is already quite late. True enough, but before that, as far back as I can recall, I was obsessed with eggs, and I still am. You cannot deny the coherence of such fixations. Those eleven years must have coincided with my incubation period. And when I turned eleven, I became a bird. Which one? Hard to say. An odd mixture of Arctic tern, cormorant, swallow and moorhen, with a touch of the common buzzard. My books are like the eggs I lay.

Among the astonishing examples of barbaric behavior displayed by the avian species, I should like to point out this one in particular: birds love to eat eggs. It is one of their favorite foods. And that is also true for me. But they prefer to eat other birds' eggs. And I can confirm that once my books no longer need my care, I prefer to read other authors'.

I n 2003, Pétronille published a magnificent novel, *The Apocalypse According to Ecuador.* It was a story about a little girl who was an incarnation of evil. Ecuador was diabolical in her own extraordinary way. Readers and critics rejoiced: while with her two previous books they could hardly have accused her of writing autobiographically, with this one they could. "Ecuador is who you were as a child, isn't she?" She would dismiss their theory with an amiable agility that only served to irritate them.

Journalists did not particularly care for this novelist who gave them no purchase on her life. To make up for this, other writers liked her a great deal. They appreciated her deeply literary temperament and her careful reading of their own works. I know something about it and I am far from being the only one who does. Pétronille established close friendships with a number of writers, including Carole Zalberg, Alain Mabanckou, Pia Petersen, and Pierrette Fleutiaux.

About her love life she revealed little. This pretty urchin broke any number of hearts, but I never found out whose. I noticed that her book signings were always attended by quite a few ravishing young women, but that by no means excluded handsome young men. Her sexual ambiguity was fascinating. The funniest thing was that several young women came and asked me for advice. These lovely things aroused my compassion. My status as drinking companion was already hard enough; I could not imagine the existential difficulty faced by these women who had fallen in love with Pétronille. So I said, "You know, Mademoiselle Fanto is not an exact science."

Although my response was cautious, I suppose it was still too daring. Because word got back to me that after a certain number of predictable disasters—affairs that were short-lived, dismissal from one day to the next—those repudiated women placed the blame on me, and held me responsible for their disappointments.

I beg to take umbrage. If there is one thing I despise more than jealousy, it is indiscretion. The attitude of these jilted *demoiselles* followed a certain logic—their pride suffered less if they imagined they had been the victims of some perverse manipulation, rather than admitting that they themselves might be a disappointment—but I found their logic perfectly inconceivable. I had enough difficulty as it was understanding my own matters of the heart; I was hardly about to go delving into other people's.

And besides, judging from the little I knew about Pétronille's morals, her behavior was not at all surprising. She herself admitted that she owed her explosive temperament to her Andorran origins. If she had been in possession of the switchblade she dreamt of, undoubtedly she would have made ample use of it. The least little thing and she flew into a rage. When I saw her lose her temper for reasons that escaped me, I tried humor to calm her down, and sometimes I succeeded. One of my methods was to say, "It's amazing how much you look like Robert De Niro in front of his mirror in *Taxi Driver*!"

When it worked, she instantly turned into Robert De Niro and said, "*You talking to me?*" with the appropriate accent. But when it didn't work, she was like some gang leader throwing endless tantrums.

"Have you quite finished pretending to be Lino Ventura in *Crooks in Clover*?" This was my final rejoinder: the name Lino Ventura was my trump card.

"Papa!" she exclaimed.

Ventura was her fantasy father. Whenever one of his films was on television, Pétronille would invite me over to her place to watch it. The moment he appeared on the screen she went into a trance.

"Don't you think he kind of looks like me?" she asked.

"There is a faint resemblance, yes."

"He's my father, I'm sure of it."

The odds that Françoise Fanto might have sinned with the famous actor back in the seventies were close to minus twenty, but as for choosing an ideal father figure, Pétronille could have done a lot worse.

In 2005, I published *Sulfuric Acid*. To date, it is my only novel that has elicited a hostile reaction. I was criticized for comparing the barbarity of certain reality TV programs with that of concentration camps. The attacks were disingenuous: my novel was set in the near future, and in no way sought to call anyone a fascist. It was pure fiction, and as such eventually things calmed down.

Nevertheless, I went through a period that, if not altogether difficult, was trying to say the least. Champagne was a precious ally, as was the young woman in my orbit.

Pétronille had just published her most exhilarating novel, *The Tough Ones*. In a way it was her version of the Hollywood masterpiece *What Ever Happened to Baby Jane?* She was right to complain that the press did not give her book enough coverage. We emptied our champagne glasses, sharing our respective disappointments.

One day, she vented her anger at me: "You just don't realize! I dream of being in your shoes!"

"Do you think it's pleasant to be insulted?"

"And to be ignored—is that any easier?"

"Don't exaggerate. Your book has not gone unnoticed."

"Oh, stop it, please. I cannot stand your pathetic

indulgence. Why don't you say it straight out: my book got what it deserved."

"And stop putting the words in my mouth. I never said that, and for good reason: it's not what I think."

"Then stop whining. You are not to be pitied."

"I'm not whining, I'm just feeling a bit disgruntled."

"Old fussbudget!"

Our squabbling gave us something in common with her characters: had we been younger, we would have been like the angry lushes she had portrayed. You can tell a writer from their immediately prophetic nature: I don't know whether my *Sulfuric Acid* turned out to be true regarding the evolution of reality television, but I am sure that her Tough Ones were incarnated in our quarrels that autumn. Which was proof, if any were needed, that Pétronille Fanto was a genuine writer.

At the end of the year, I found this message on my voice-mail: "Bird, get out your best champagne. I'll be at your place tomorrow at six in the evening. I have some news for you."

I immediately put a 1976 Dom Pérignon on ice. What did she have to tell me? Had she met someone? Was she in love?

She luxuriated in the first sip and told me that she would miss it.

"Are you going to stop drinking?" I asked, alarmed.

"After a fashion. I'm going away."

"Where?"

She made a vague gesture as if sweeping her hand over vast territories.

"I'm going to cross the Sahara desert on foot."

Coming from anyone else, a statement like this would

have made me laugh out loud. But Pétronille did not have a drop of indecisiveness in her blood, and I knew she really intended to go through with her rash scheme.

"Whatever for?" I stammered.

"I must. If I stay here any longer, I'll be infected by the filthy mannerisms of the literati."

"But you can avoid that. Look at me, I haven't got them."

"You're not normal. It's something I need to do, really. I don't want to go stale."

"You, go stale? That's impossible."

"I just turned thirty."

You would never have known. She hardly seemed a day older than when we first met and I thought she was fifteen. She looked seventeen.

"How long will you be gone?"

"Who knows."

"Will you come back?"

"Yes."

"Are you sure?"

As if in reply, she reached into her bag and handed me a parcel.

"I'm entrusting you with my latest manuscript. It's valuable. I'm totally fed up with publishers. If you think it deserves to be published, then please look into it. I'm proud of this manuscript and I have every intention of assuming my parental role. So you can consider it proof of my return."

Only with great effort did I take a sip of the best champagne on earth.

"I'm grateful you haven't offered to come with me," she said.

"I'm like you: I never come out and make statements regarding things I don't think I'll go through with. To be sure, crossing the Sahara on foot is bound to be sublime, but it's not my thing. When are you leaving?"

"Tomorrow."

"Excuse me?"

"I've got to. Otherwise, I'll start having this literati attitude: I'll be waiting to hear what you think of my manuscript."

"I can read it tonight."

"No. I know you: you never read when you're drunk."

"What makes you think I'll be drunk?" I asked, raising the flute to my lips.

She laughed, her marvelous radiantly healthy laugh.

"I'll miss you," I said.

My chin was trembling.

"You're so sentimental!" she exclaimed, rolling her eyes.

And indeed, I belong to the race of those who weep when their friends go away and don't know when they'll be coming back. I have a long experience of separation, and I know better than anyone what is at risk: when you leave someone and promise you'll meet again, this can be an omen of the most terrible things. Most often, you never see the person in question again. And that is not the worst thing that can happen. The worst is when you do see the person again and you don't recognize them: either they've truly changed a great deal, or you find that they have some incredibly unpleasant characteristic they must have always had, but you had managed to blind yourself to it, in the name of that strange sort of love which is so mysterious and so dangerous and where you never quite know what is at stake: friendship.

Sentimentality needs fuel. We had to open a second bottle. When I sensed that I would soon stop being presentable, I threw Pétronille out.

Through the window, I watched her fragile little figure walk away into the night. Tears were pouring down my cheeks.

"How will I manage without you, you monkey?" I wailed.

I went and collapsed on the bed, more dead than alive.

In the morning when I'd finished my writing, I opened my fugitive friend's parcel and saw the title of her manuscript: *I Cannot Feel My Strength.* "That certainly is true," I thought. I immediately started reading. I prefer not to say anything about the book other than: if ever a text deserved to be called "awe-inspiring," this is the one.

I would have to contact publishers about the novel in Miss Fanto's place. It would be no easy thing. "Good old Pétronille! You've only just left, and you're already a bigger pain than when you were here."

I am someone who keeps her promises. That very afternoon I photocopied the manuscript and sent it out to various publishers, leaving my name and address. As far as the French publishing industry was concerned, the results were both laudatory and disgraceful. The fact that my name made things go considerably faster was to be expected. The fact that all those publishers turned down such a beautiful and risky text was shameful. But I might point out that none of them suspected me of writing the manuscript. Which proves one remarkable and reassuring thing: people in this town still know how to read.

I would not admit defeat for all that. Since mailing out

the manuscript had been fruitless, I would go and deliver the manuscript to the next batch of publishers in person. The fact that I was making the effort to go there in person would reflect the depth of my conviction.

And that is what I did. A great number of appointments followed: they were all stunned to see me, because I am reputed to be as loyal to my publisher, Albin Michel, as Penelope was to Ulysses. I quickly disappointed them with my announcement that it was not a text of my own that was the purpose of my visit.

"Do you do this for many authors?" they asked.

"This is a first, and will no doubt remain the only time."

Then I had to wait for their verdict.

I, too, happened to be a writer and a human being. So I went on writing and living.

The hardest thing was finding another drinking companion. Worst luck, the marvelous Théodora, who drank so gracefully, chose that moment to pull up stakes and move to Taiwan. For me, 2006 was much the same as it had been for Pétronille: a crossing of the desert.

And anyway, this was no time for pleasure. Through my intervention, Pétronille's manuscript was accumulating one rejection after another, and this was getting me down. One nice young female editor even wrote to me and said point-blank: "Why are you going to all this trouble for this Fanto woman? You know very well that in the literary world, people with a proletarian background don't stand a chance."

I could never have made up such a remark, and it left me speechless. If I'm relaying it here, it is because I do not want to hide the fact that in Paris, in 2006, a person wrote to me to point out such a thing in all seriousness. I leave it to others to make of it what they will.

When I started feeling truly dejected, I took comfort in thinking, "What if an editor actually accepts the manuscript then asks to meet the author? You'll be obliged to say that Pétronille Fanto is in the Sahara desert for an unspecified length of time, and the contract would be deferred, and thus immediately forgotten. It's enough to set you to grinding your teeth, isn't it? It's better this way."

And I had my own novels to stick up for. My Italian publisher sent me to a book signing in Venice, and I arrived right in the middle of the Carnival. People in the street congratulated me on my disguise; I was simply wearing my work clothes. There was some controversy over my hat, which according to the French was that of a nonjuring priest, but the Italians insisted that it was the same that was worn by plague-era physicians.

That autumn I watched the wild geese migrating. "Pétronille, when you coming back?" Needless to say, I had no news. Perhaps she was dead. At the same time, as I still hadn't found her a publisher. It was just as well she wasn't here.

I read a text Rimbaud wrote just before he disappeared: *"I shall come back, with limbs of iron, dark skin, and a vengeful eye: from my mask, it will be said I belong to a strong race. I will have gold: I will be indolent and brutal."*

These splendid words resonated curiously with me. Would I ever see Pétronille again? And if I did, what sort of state would she be in?

In November, I found a drinking companion worthy of the name in the person of Nathanaëlle, a young friend who had just moved to Paris. She was totally reliable, which is the most important characteristic for this position: after several flutes of champagne, you are bound to unveil a few secrets. By definition, trust must be absolute, therefore you can count on one hand the people you can trust.

The second-most important characteristic of the drinking companions is that they must not turn up their noses at the bubbly. Otherwise, you are left with the impression that you are drinking on your own, which is precisely what you had wanted to avoid.

Thirdly, drinking companions must be happy drinkers: they are not there to divulge their bitterness. Nathanaëlle turned out to be ideal. In this matter as in all others, the point is not to replace someone: no one can replace another person. But life became more lighthearted.

The editorial curse only lasted through 2006. At the end of January, 2007, I received a favorable response from Fayard regarding Pétronille's manuscript. My joy was even greater than when my own first novel was accepted by Albin Michel. *All that is missing is the author's presence for everything to be perfect*, I thought.

As the letter from Fayard stipulated that they would like to meet Mademoiselle Fanto, I had begun entertaining the idea of hiring an actress who looked like her to play her part, when the telephone rang:

"It's Pétronille."

"Pétro! Are you calling from the desert?"

"No, I'm at the Gare Montparnasse. Come and get me, I've forgotten how things work here."

I rushed to the station, expecting to find the reincarnation of Lawrence of Arabia. She was merely dark brown, thinner, with wild eyes, but recognizable.

"Hi there, bird."

"Where do you want to go? Home?"

"I don't know. Where do I live?"

While the taxi took us to the twentieth arrondissement, I urged her to tell me all about it. She hardly said a thing.

"It's January 31," I said. "You've been gone for more than a year. Did you enjoy it?"

"More than that. Much more than that!"

Fortunately, I had kept a set of her keys, because she no longer had her own. She gazed around her apartment as if in a stupor.

"It's going to be strange not sleeping under the stars."

A pile of bills and other mail awaited, which the concierge had slipped under the door. Pétronille picked it all up and threw it into the trash. I intervened: "And your taxes?"

"I wasn't in France in 2006. If they don't like it, they can put me in jail. I'm hungry. What do people eat in this country?"

At the corner bistro, I ordered her some salt pork with lentils, so she would become reacclimatized to her biotope. Then I told her the big news:

"I've found a publisher for your manuscript."

"Oh, right," she answered, as if this were the most normal thing in the world.

And as I knew how hard it had been, I was somewhat put out. I was tempted to tell her about the repeated humiliation I had suffered on her behalf. But I decided against it, because it was too unpleasant. And she might have been so disgusted that she would have turned around and gone straight back to the Sahara.

The worst thing is that I understood her: the fact that her novel had found a publisher was indeed the most normal thing in the world.

"What was it called already, my manuscript?"

"*I Cannot Feel My Strength.*"

"I cannot feel my strength? That's certainly true."

"You should reread it. Fayard want to meet you."

"There's no rush."

"Yes, there is. I made an appointment for you on February 6."

This wasn't true, but her offhand behavior was beginning to annoy me.

Our food arrived. Pétronille began eating the lentils with her hands.

"Now you're going too far," I said.

"The Tuaregs," she said, absently.

"Obviously. But if, by some miracle, the publisher invites you to lunch on February 6, use your knife and fork."

That afternoon I ordered her to bed, although she claimed that she now slept on the floor, and I called Fayard to make an appointment for February 6.

I spent the days that followed breathlessly dreading that Pétronille might behave disastrously during the appointment.

On February 6, in the evening, she called me to assure me that she had put her best foot forward. As that could mean anything, I asked her whether she had signed a contract.

"Who do you take me for? Of course I did. My book will come out in the autumn, like yours."

I immediately invited her over to celebrate, and noted with relief that at least the Tuaregs had not managed to put her off champagne.

The desert remained a mystery. When I tried to get Pétronille to talk about it, she dodged the issue. One day I provoked her.

"You never went to the Sahara. For thirteen months you hid out in Palavas-les-Flots."

"If that was the case, I would bore you with stories about the desert."

One evening as we were starting on the second bottle of an excellent Dom-Ruinart blanc de blancs, she confessed that she had been sleeping very badly.

"Ever since I got back," she said. "I can't stand this urban racket anymore."

"Your neighborhood is not that noisy."

"But it is, compared to the Sahara. You have no idea of the silence there. What I liked best of all about the desert was the nighttime. I would pitch my tent as far away as possible from the Tuaregs. You don't know what silence is if you've never heard that silence."

"Wasn't it frightening?"

"Anything but. There is nothing more restful. I slept like an angel. Sometimes I would wake up, nature calling. The sand was so white, so luminous, it was like walking in snow. Overhead, this unbelievable sky, a profusion of stars, bigger and brighter, like constellations from a hundred thousand years ago. I could have wept with joy."

"No snakes?"

"I didn't see any. In the morning, I would go back to the caravan. The men baked bread in the sand. It was wonderful. I don't know why I came back here."

"To drink champagne with me."

"Quite a job."

"That it is. You have to be strong."

Even though she didn't talk about it, she must have been pleased when *I Cannot Feel My Strength* was published. The novel garnered the admiration of the happy few. And these happy few included my father.

"Nietzsche has been reborn," he said. "Who is this author?"

After giving it some thought, I decided that Patrick Nothomb—a man who had shot the breeze with rebels who were armed to the teeth, and drunk tea in the company of Chairman Mao—would be up to meeting Pétronille.

My parents invited us to lunch in Brussels. My mother, who simply cannot get her titles right, congratulated her guest on her book *May You Find The Strength.*

"Have you read it, Maman?" I asked her sotto voce.

"I have. I didn't understand what it was supposed to mean, but it was very beautiful."

In the meantime my father, somewhat awkwardly but with dignity, was explaining to Pétronille why her book was a masterpiece. I saw that she was impressed. She had an expression on her face that I had never seen.

Once we sat down to lunch, my mother asked her about her background.

"I grew up in the banlieue of Paris," she said.

All my parents knew about France was what they saw on the news, and they gave her a horrified look. Pétronille must have realized that they thought she was a kid from the projects, and she did nothing to correct their misapprehension.

I joined in her game: "Did you set many cars on fire?"

"I stopped when I turned thirteen."

"You moved on to other things?"

"Yeah. My gang started doing crack. That's when I decided it was time to split, and I began reading Shakespeare."

My parents' admiration for the Bard soared to incredible heights.

On the train on our way home, I burst out laughing.

"What on earth were you playing at?"

"You have no idea. Your father really intimidated me. I wanted to live up to his expectations."

"That you did. But the naked truth shows you in an even better light, if you want my opinion."

"Isn't your mother a little peculiar?"

"Don't worry about her. She says the title of my most famous novel is *Cries and Whispers.*"

I was convinced that Pétronille's next book would be about the desert. I was wrong: in early 2009 *Love on an Empty Stomach* was published. It was the tale of a fortune hunter in the American South in the early twentieth century.

It was an adventure novel, and it was a real hit. She appeared on a literary program, and attracted the attention of Jacques Chessex. The great Swiss writer was clearly taken with this human stick of dynamite, and he sent her a stunning letter of the kind only he could write:

Dear Pétronille Fanto,

Your novel has confirmed what I saw with my own eyes: you are a child and you are an ogre.

You are now one of my jesters.

Jacques Chessex

I was struck by the cogency of his words. The fact that this man who was an expert on ogres (had his novel *The Ogre* not won the Prix Goncourt?) had branded Pétronille an ogre served as a warning to me.

"He's right," I said. "When I spend time with you, I feel as if I'm being devoured."

"You don't seem to mind. But why did he say I was a child?"

"Ask him."

It was a delicate topic. We didn't dare tell her that at the age of thirty-four she looked eighteen.

I don't know if she ever asked Chessex, but their correspondence flourished. When that autumn the Swiss author died, Pétronille mourned him the way a daughter mourns a father.

When I saw her swollen face—but swollen only on one side—I couldn't believe she had wept all that profusely.

"Have you had cosmetic surgery? Is that the secret of your eternal youth?"

"No."

"What's the matter with you? Please tell me."

"I'm taking part in clinical trials for pharmaceutical companies."

"You are? Why?"

"To make money."

"Is it legal?"

"Sort of."

"You're crazy, Pétro!"

"Believe it or not, it's hardly my royalties that'll pay my bills."

"Have you looked at yourself in the mirror? You look like half of one of the Bogdanov brothers."

"It will go away."

"Are you sure?"

"Yes. It's Bromboramase, for gastroenteritis."

"Just looking like that is enough to give anyone instantaneous gastroenteritis!"

"You're such a fussbudget. Good job you didn't see me last week, after the Gascalgine 30H. It's medication for improving blood circulation."

"And?"

"My face was so swollen around my eyelids I couldn't open my eyes. I'm not exaggerating: for two days I was technically blind."

"I hope the lab paid you overtime."

"As long as it's only my body, I don't mind."

"What do you mean?"

"When the side effects start affecting your brain it's not so funny. A month ago I tested this thing for postpartum depression. I understood after it was over why it worked: I lost all my recent memory. Imagine, you have this mother who has just given birth, and she doesn't even remember being pregnant. When she sees her baby, she wonders who it is."

"And so what happened with you?"

"I couldn't remember anything that had happened since I came back from the desert. The memory loss lasted several days."

"Pétronille, please, stop this evil work."

"And how am I supposed to eat?"

"I can give you some money."

"Are you out of your mind? I'm a free woman."

Under normal circumstances, I would have found her declaration hilarious. But now it went straight to my heart: could this crazy kid be trusted to look after herself?

"Aren't you afraid there will be lasting consequences?" I asked.

"I'm a very brave person."

"Recklessly so."

"And besides, I'm having fun. There's a sorcerer's apprentice side to it—you never know what's going to happen."

"You don't need to go playing sorcerer's apprentice. *Love on an Empty Stomach* is doing well."

"You only get royalties after a whole year has gone by, in case you'd forgotten."

"Ask for an advance. Your editor will get it for you."

"I have my dignity."

"It's misguided."

"Leave me alone, bird. Who do you think you are, telling me how to behave? You spend all your royalties on champagne!"

"Well, given how you help me drink it, you shouldn't complain. What's more, is your medication compatible with alcohol?"

"Leave me alone."

I started to be really worried. I began calling Pétronille every day. When it comes to people I care for, I have a mother hen side I cannot control. In the case in point, I think it was warranted. Before long, she stopped picking up when she saw my number on the screen. This did little to reassure me.

In November, at the book fair in Brive, I thought Pétronille was behaving oddly. I told her so.

"Have you seen the way you're looking at me? That's why I act strange," she replied.

"I'm not so sure."

"In what way am I behaving strangely, then?"

"You laugh all the time, and you're constantly eating."

"Yes. It's called the book fair in Brive-la-Gaillarde."

Perhaps she was right. But the following month she was the one who called me one night at around midnight.

"What proof is there that I am not you?" she said. "There is no border between human beings. Amélie, I feel physically like the champagne you drank this evening."

"The medication you're testing at the moment, it wouldn't be LSD, would it?"

"I'm looking out at Paris through the window: did you know that the Eiffel Tower is hollow? It's a launchpad for rockets."

"You're confusing it with Kourou in French Guiana."

"That's for the space shuttle. The Eiffel Tower is for private rockets. With an orbital speed of eleven kilometers per second, you can leave the Earth's atmosphere very quickly."

"Are you calling me for help?"

"No. I just wanted to let you know that I'm coming with you. I can't let you go into space on your own, I've seen the way you slice lemons. But for pity's sake, take off those orange pajamas, the color makes me want to throw up."

"I'm on my way."

Words cannot describe the anxiety I felt during the ride to her apartment. I went up the stairs four at a time and found Pétronille in the middle of frying fish.

"You want some?" she asked, as natural as can be.

She slid the fish from the frying pan onto her plate and started eating.

"You eat fish at one o'clock in the morning?"

"Sure. Don't make such a face. It's perfectly legal."

The smell was not reassuring. While she was stuffing her face, I looked around the kitchen: the mess beggared belief. A bachelor pad.

"Don't you ever wish you were part of a couple?"

"Are you off your head?" she replied, indignant, with her mouth full.

"What's wrong with asking?"

"You know very well that I can't stand anyone."

"And that no one can stand you?"

"That's not my problem. I am enchanted with my freedom."

I noticed a blister pack of pills and reached for it: "Extrabromelanase…Is that what makes you so free that you called me at midnight?"

"If it bothers you so much you shouldn't pick up."

"But I'm worried sick about you! When I see your number, I pick up. And with what you've been telling me, I have every reason to panic. What is this stuff supposed to treat, anyway?"

"It stabilizes schizophrenics."

"Pétronille, I forbid you from taking one more pill. You must write a report, immediately, about this medication, and specify its very grave side effects."

"Don't exaggerate."

"What do you want?"

"I'm young, I like danger, and I love the Russian roulette side of this job which, I might mention, is well-paid. So there."

"You could die, you know."

"I know. That's why I said Russian roulette."

"And what about me? Have you thought about me?"

"You can live without me."

"I can. But not as well. How selfish you are! And besides, even if you don't die, you might be left with terrible irreversible aftereffects."

"And what do you suggest?"

"Find another way to earn your living."

"I've tried. I've been a waitress, a school supervisor, an English tutor. It was all dead boring and didn't leave me the time to write. Do you know that you are one of the rare privileged individuals who actually lives from her writing? One percent of the writers who are published actually manage to live from their trade. One percent!"

"It's the finest profession on earth. You cannot expect it to be easy."

"Well, you make it look easy. I had always dreamt of being a writer, but it was seeing you that convinced me I should go ahead and try. People figure that if you can do it, so can they."

"And they're right."

"They're wrong: it's not a question of talent. I've watched you: I'm not saying you don't have talent, but I am saying, because I've studied you for a long time, that talent is not enough. The secret is your craziness."

"You are a thousand times crazier than I am, with or without your medication!"

"It's *your* craziness, I said: it's your particular way of being crazy. There are crazy people everywhere. But crazy people like you—they don't exist. No one knows just what goes to make up your craziness. Not even you."

"That's true."

"And that's why it's a scam. Because of you people become writers, but they don't realize that they don't have—not one of them—your fuel at their disposal."

"So? Do you regret it? You've written wonderful novels!"

"I don't regret a thing. But allow me to ruin my health, since that's the price I have to pay."

"In that case, don't expect me to be your witness. Don't call me at midnight to tell me that the Eiffel Tower is a launchpad for private rockets."

"I did that?"

"Why do you think I'm here? We have a problem, Pétronille. To leave you in that state is tantamount to a failure to render assistance to a person in danger. Come and stay at my place."

"Stay at your place? Hell on earth."

"Thank you very much."

"I promise I won't call you at midnight anymore. You can go now."

In early January, 2010, I got a call from the Cochin hospital:

"We have a patient here, Peronilla Fanto, who has assured us that you would be willing to put her up for a while."

"What's wrong with her?"

"It's a mystery. She has developed allergies to… all sorts of things. She can't stay on her own at the moment."

Thus, a major trauma victim came to stay with me.

"There you go, getting yourself another ride in an ambulance," I said.

"It's not funny."

"You're right. You're not going to test any more drugs?"

"Never again."

She didn't want to tell me what had happened. It seemed to have reached unthinkable proportions.

Our cohabitation and lasted nearly three months. She turned out to be difficult. Pétronille could not stand dust, or the color orange, or the smell of cheese, or my dried flowers, or my music ("God they're awful, your Gothic hymns!"), or my lifestyle ("I thought you were Belgian, but you're German!"—I never found out what she meant by that).

Personally, I found she had changed. Her intolerance

toward that unknown drug had left her in a state of shock: she had become a hypochondriac, ultrasensitive to noise and to the oddest things, like M&Ms, or my painting of sunflowers in the snow, my deodorant, the chandelier in the kitchen ("I don't believe it, a chandelier in the kitchen!"). And finally, she didn't get along with my cacti. Even drinking champagne with her was not as pleasant as it used to be. She seemed constantly on edge, and abnormally vulnerable. We often argued for the most incomprehensible reasons.

One day I made the mistake of cursing the pill that had changed her. It lit the powder keg: Pétronille left and took her belongings with her. I knew I must never bring up that subject again.

Nothing new under the sun: just because you adore someone doesn't mean you can necessarily live with them. As usual, for weeks Pétronille gave no sign of life. But our friendship had known many such periods of silence. During this one, I thought of her with a warlike pride. Pétronille was like a glorious soldier who had not tried to protect herself and who, when she came back from combat battered and victorious, went straight back to the front of literature.

In this era of pretentious young women, where the word "violence" is bandied left and right, here was a young novelist who had exposed her body to a real danger in order to continue writing. In a very singular way she had illustrated the book by Michel Leiris, *On Literature as a Form of Bullfighting*, associating the act of writing with authentic danger, thus endowing it with laurels that had previously become irrelevant.

When Pétronille was in one of her moods, I left the initiative to her. She contacted me several months later to tell me she had a novel coming out with Flammarion, and that she was now working as a literary critic for a major weekly publication in Luxembourg. I was completely taken aback by this last piece of news.

"What's the connection between you and Luxembourg? Do you have a secret bank account there?"

"You know very well I have no money."

True enough. I knew no one who was so broke. One day I saw her with holes in her socks, and I suggested we go buy some new ones; she answered that all she had to do was layer several pairs. "Socks never get holes in the same place," she said philosophically.

"But how did you land such a prestigious position?" I pressed her.

"It's too complicated to explain."

Pétronille's life was awash with mystery. This adventurer in the world of writing was not without savoir-faire. Before long her literary column was being read by a good number of French people, who were impressed by the independence of her opinions and the elegance of her style. She became a respected authority.

There is the danger, in such a position, of it becoming stultifyingly routine. Many people would have taken advantage of the situation to play the literary luminary. Her novel *The Distribution of Shadows* won a prestigious literary prize—as did her previous novel—and this was something any other writer would have boasted about ad nauseam. Pétronille didn't even seem to notice.

It was the following year, I think, that it began. It's hard to describe a phenomenon you know practically nothing about.

It seemed that Pétronille had fallen in love. But I cannot be sure.

In love with whom? That I know even less. And was it going well? I have no idea.

As she was once again my drinking companion, when she was as drunk as I was I would grill her, but to no avail. The champagne made her open up about a great number of subjects, but not that one.

It did not stop her from writing, for all that. Love is not known for causing inspiration to dry up.

In 2012, she published the finest apocalyptic novel I know, *The Immediate*. Then she came out with a fantasy fiction about tattoos, *The Blood of Sorrow*. Although it wasn't patently obvious, each of these books, in its way, was a love story.

Pétronille went traveling. She left for Budapest. She disappeared to New York. She said that, like Frédéric Moreau in Flaubert's *Sentimental Education*, she wanted to become acquainted with "the melancholy of ocean liners."

"You went to New York on an ocean liner?" I asked, astonished.

"What matters is having the impression that I did," she answered enigmatically.

At the beginning of 2014, I got wind of an affair so incredible that I refused to believe it: I heard that, several nights a week, in so-called nocturnal circles, Pétronille was performing an act of Russian roulette.

I laughed until I could laugh no more, and thought about calling the performer herself, just in order to apprise her of the rumors going around—"Unto those that have shall more be given," I would have said—when she called me:

"I can't make it on Thursday evening."

"Which Thursday evening? Next Thursday?"

"March 20."

"But it's your birthday."

"I've got work."

"You have work on the evening of your birthday?"

"It can't be helped."

"You promised we'd spend the evening together!"

"Don't insist."

She hung up. I was in a foul mood. I tried to persuade myself that it was because of one of her strange amorous trysts: "But then why did she have such a sinister tone of voice?" I wondered.

The rumor I'd heard maintained that Pétronille was performing her Russian roulette act in a cellar on the rue

Saint-Sabin. Since I now had nothing planned for the evening of March 20, there was nothing to stop me spending it in the cellar in question.

On the appointed day, I arrived at the place at around seven in the evening, dressed like a vivandière from the Holy Grail, which did not set me apart from the other patrons.

"Poor Pétronille, you must really be desperate for cash to agree to work in such a smoky dive!" I thought.

In a waterproof backpack filled with ice cubes I had a bottle of champagne, a Joseph-Perrier blanc de blancs vintage 2002, with a flute in each side pocket. This was an inspired move, because the menu of the Saint-Sabin cellar offered only beer and spiced wine.

There were no posters advertising any Russian roulette numbers—either to avoid problems in the event of a police raid, or because the whole business was just a fabrication, I thought.

The vaulted ceiling must have dated back to the catacombs, the lighting would have been perfect for a clandestine burial, the patrons and waiters were sporting skulls on every finger—everything here was an omen of death. I began to feel more and more uncomfortable.

Then I heard a lovely song that my brain took some time to identify: *Roulette*, by System of a Down. People reacted to this signal by falling silent. As there was neither a stage nor a podium, it was in front of the bar that I saw

Pétronille arrive, and for the first time she seemed tall to me, perhaps because she was the only one standing up. From her jeans pocket she took a revolver and began a long-winded speech in a high-pitched and intelligible voice.

"Ladies and gentlemen, Russian Roulette is a game that never goes out of fashion…"

I had already stopped listening. Bloody hell, so it was true! Fear, pure and simple, quickly gave way to panic, so much so that I was literally petrified.

For the benefit of anyone who did not know the rules, Pétronille opened her weapon, displayed the empty cylinder, placed a single bullet in it, snapped it shut then spun the cylinder, the act which had given the venerable gun its name. To conclude her spiel she said, "Are there any volunteers present?"

The audience burst out laughing. Not I.

"You can only ever count on yourself, as always."

The song by System of a Down was over.

"And now I will ask you to remain silent."

She had no trouble obtaining their silence. You could hear the cylinder spinning, or at least you thought you heard it, since everyone was so riveted on what was unfolding before their eyes. Pétronille placed the barrel against her temple and said, "Dostoyevsky, who had been sentenced to death and didn't know he would be pardoned at the last minute, tells of his experience before the firing squad—the seconds that seemed to last a dizzyingly long time, the insane beauty of the tiniest little thing, his eyes opening at last to see what he must see. Now from my own position, I can confirm that he was right."

She pressed the trigger. Nothing happened.

I was about to go on my knees to thank Providence when she said, "In westerns they call this thing a six-shooter. So I will shoot it six times. Only five more to go!"

As she began to repeat the operation, I recalled something from very long ago: a video that had been making the rounds about ten years earlier, *Russian Roulette Made Easy,* or something of that ilk, in which an expert gave instruction in the decisive gesture, the one you had to make to spin the cylinder in order to determine where the bullet would end up. Might Pétronille have learned this technique? I hoped so.

She pressed the trigger. Nothing.

"Only four more," she declared.

I watched carefully as she spun the cylinder: her gesture was perfect, insofar as you could not detect any deliberate intention. I would not be granted the key to the mystery.

"The barrel knows the way to my temple now," she said.

She pressed the trigger. Nothing.

"Only three left."

Even if she had seen that video, the risk Pétronille was taking was nevertheless enormous. Even seasoned prestidigitators could make mistakes, so all the more reason for an adventurer like her to make one.

She pressed the trigger. Nothing.

"Just two more."

Only Pétronille still maintained her composure. The entire room was in a trance, and me most of all. What we were experiencing and expressing through our heightened silence was of a genre beyond fear, a sort of becalmed climax—time had stood still, every second was divisible unto infinity, we were all Dostoyevsky facing the firing squad, and it was on our temple that we could feel the tip of the gun barrel.

She pressed the trigger. Nothing.

"Only one more."

A sudden flash of understanding went through me from head to toe: what had made me feel so close to Pétronille right from the start was this very sensation, this intoxication which for lack of a better word we call a love of risk, which does not obey any biological instinct or rational analysis, and which I had illustrated in a less spectacular but no less definitive way in circumstances that are unprintable. We were clearly not in the majority, to be sure, in this golden age of the principle of caution, and we understood each other all the better for it. How could I have ever begun to imagine she might be performing this act for money? And how could she have insisted on the fact that she was testing those drugs for profit? If Pétronille had placed herself—and was placing herself again—in such danger, it was in order to experience the supreme exaltation and ecstatic dilation of feeling truly alive.

She pressed the trigger. Nothing.

As the audience had already begun shouting, she motioned to us to be quiet and said:

"Don't go thinking I've been taking you for a ride."

And without spinning the barrel, she took aim at a bottle on top of the counter and fired. The shot was so loud that you could hardly hear the glass breaking.

A thundering round of applause. Resplendent, Pétronille came over to the table where I was sitting on my own, and sat down next to me.

"Bravo! You were magnificent!" I was exultant.

"Do you think so?" she said with false modesty.

"And what an original way to celebrate your thirty-ninth birthday! Is it an allusion to Hitchcock's *39 Steps*?"

"Enough chatter. What are we drinking?"

"I have just what we need," I answered, pulling out a bottle of champagne.

I filled the flutes and raised a toast to her glorious exploit. The first sip enthralled me: nothing improves the taste of champagne like Russian roulette.

"You almost had to drink without me," said Pétronille.

"You have given me the opportunity to put one of Napoleon's mottos into practice: he always had a bottle of champagne on ice, to drink after the battle. 'If I am victorious, I deserve it, but if I am defeated, I need it,' he said."

"And what is your verdict?"

"You deserve it. Happy birthday."

As usual, I spoke too soon. Late in the night, we quarreled about god knows what, and the alcohol made it seem all the more important. At that point we were walking down the Boulevard Richard-Lenoir, and Pétronille, ever an irrepressible personality, slid a bullet into the cylinder and spun it around as she saw fit. She put the barrel against my temple and fired.

"This time, it's not Marlowe who has departed this life in a street brawl," she said to my corpse.

She rummaged in my bag, found this manuscript, which she put in her pocket, and threw my body into the Canal Saint-Martin.

The next day was a Friday, a workday. To ease her conscience, Pétronille took the manuscript to my publisher.

"It's not very long," she told him. "I'll stick around, you read it, and then we'll talk about it."

In the meantime she settled into my office where, in her typical offhand manner, she made a phone call lasting two and a half hours to Timbuktu.

After that, the publisher came to ask her whether she oughtn't, rather, take the manuscript to the police.

"I'll let you be the judge of that," she replied.

Pétronille dashed off like a cat and vanished onto the roofs of Paris, where I'll wager she is still prowling about to this day.

As for me, like a well-behaved stiff I have been meditating at the bottom of the canal, and the lessons I have learned from this affair will be of no use. Even though I know that writing is dangerous, and one can risk one's life in the process, I always fall for it.

About the Author

Amélie Nothomb was born in Japan of Belgian parents in 1967. She lives in Paris. Since her debut on the French literary scene, she has published a novel a year, every year. Her ebullient fiction, unconventional thinking, and public persona have combined to transform her into a worldwide literary sensation. Her books have been translated into over twenty-five languages and been awarded numerous prizes including the French Academy's 1999 Grand Prix of the Novel, the René-Fallet prize, the Alain-Fournier prize, and the Grand Prix Giono in 2008.